BEWARE STALKING KILLERS

"Out by the camel path! There's a dead man!"

The body was lying on its back on our side of the camel path, nearly hidden in the tall, dense grasses, and had been horribly trampled and mutilated. The skull was broken, half the face smashed, but the clothes and remaining features were recognizable. The dead man was Richard Cartwright.

"His head looks more likely done with a rock from the stone wall than the foot of a hippopotamus."

The police captain gave a wry smile. "I fear my hopes got the better of my wits," he admitted. The murderer is still among us, but now he has claimed *two* victims."

———————— ★ ————————

HILLARY WAUGH

THE RECIPIENT OF THE 1989 MYSTERY WRITERS OF AMERICA GRAND MASTER AWARD

MURDER ON
SAFARI

HILLARY WAUGH

WORLDWIDE.

TORONTO · NEW YORK · LONDON · PARIS
AMSTERDAM · STOCKHOLM · HAMBURG
ATHENS · MILAN · TOKYO · SYDNEY

MURDER ON SAFARI

A Worldwide Mystery/August 1989

First published by Dodd, Mead & Company, Inc.

ISBN 0-373-26029-6

Printed in U.S.A.

To Shannon,
the Golden Girl who lights up my life

ONE

MY NAME IS James Addison. That won't mean anything to most people, though some of you may have seen my byline. In the newspaper business, you start as a reporter. If you get good enough, they'll start printing your name at the head of your stories. If you feel, as I did, that the strictures laid on reporters are too confining, that it's not writing in the creative sense, you try to move on into article writing. There you have some freedom. You can express yourself without being guilty of "coloration." It's a step toward what I really wanted to do: write a detective story—which is what this is, except that this one really happened.

I have to explain that a little.

The writing bug didn't bite me until I was well out of college. English was my major back then, and an English major who doesn't want to teach graduates into a dearth of opportunities. My first job was as a reader in a New York publishing house, a low-paying, low-esteem occupation, a far cry from the onward and upward careers my classmates, who'd had the good sense to major in engineering, economics, business administration, and the like, found awaiting *them* upon graduation.

If you're a *good* reader, you get some of the better stuff to look at, manuscripts submitted by agents, manuscripts turned in by writers who've been published before, writers who have learned how to write.

And I happened to read the manuscript of Jesse Dakar's fourth mystery novel, all four of which, as most of you know, were made into movies, for which Jesse Dakar wrote the screenplays. He was very big for a few years, but it wasn't his success that impressed me, it was the way he wrote. He was the one who seized me with the desire to write myself.

But readers don't write. If I wanted to write, I had to go where writing was done. So I became a reporter. And when I decided that reporting was good training, but it wasn't really writing, I worked at convincing my editor I should do articles.

I did articles. I've done them on stained glass, on poultry raising, on the traffic problem in New York. At my own suggestion, I did one on readers in publishing houses, on the pros and cons of New York as a bachelor's paradise, on the rise and fall and rise again of the mystery novel.

It was because of this that my editor, his name is Bill Clayborn, called me into his office a few weeks ago and said to me, "Do you like animals, Jim?"

"Sure," I said. He's a large, scowling man and if this were a TV series, I'd cast Ed Asner in the role. He sits behind a big desk and he's always fishing for the particular paper he wants. He calls you into his office for something, then has to hunt and sort through the litter to find the something he wanted to talk to you about. He has a reputation for being efficient but he doesn't make his minions efficient. Like the Army, we hurry up and wait.

"It's in here somewhere," he said, and I thought he was going to send me to the ASPCA.

Finally he came up with it. "The Bird Watchers Society," he cribbed from the sheet, "is announcing a safari in Africa. Two weeks in Kenya starting June nineteenth, returning to New York, July third."

"And you want an article?"

"For the travel section, and you're damned right I want it." He leaned forward with his rolled shirt-sleeved elbows on the desk. "Do you want to know something? Mankind is eventually going to wipe out every other species of creature in existence, except cockroaches and mosquitoes. Cockroaches and mosquitoes have us over a barrel. But you watch out, everything else that we don't keep either for pets or to eat, like cats, dogs, pork, beef, and chicken, is going the way of the dinosaur and the woolly mammoth." He jabbed a finger at a spot on the paper. "Do you want to know something? There are only four rhinoceroses—rhinoceri?—you name it, in the Kenya game parks? And the gamekeepers drive around in Jeeps all day trying to keep track of where they are to keep them from getting killed by poachers. And do you know why poachers sneak into the park, at risk of life and limb, to try to kill those rhinocer—those rhinos? Because a bunch of stupid Chinese jerks believe powdered rhinoceros horn is an aphrodisiac! Now that's not so, it is not an aphrodisiac—and I'm not speaking from experience, only from plain common sense. But you can't teach plain common sense to a Chinaman. You can't teach it to a lot of the people in our own country, for that matter. Most people in the world are not born smart. You can tell they aren't because they think they *are*. That's a sure sign!

"What I'm saying is, powdered rhinoceros horn in China is like cocaine in America. People will pay anything to get it. Only the reason is different. And if people will pay for something, other people will sell it to them, and if the price is right, sellers will risk their lives to satisfy the need. That means that, in my educated opinion, there won't be any more powdered rhinoceros horn being sold on the streets of China by the year 2000 because there won't be any rhinos left." He looked me straight in the eye. "Have you ever seen a rhinoceros?"

"In the zoo."

"They'll get them, too."

He scowled at the sheet and threw it aside. "And that's not all," he went on. "Elephants. They're doomed, too. Not as soon as the rhino, but soon. And seals. And whales. You name it. So, if you want to see these animals in their native habitat, not behind bars of a cage, like your rhino, you got to go out there fast. I mean fast."

I said, "Like tomorrow?"

"Like June nineteenth!" He struck the paper with his fist. "Weren't you listening to me? June nineteenth, and back July third."

I said, "That's the day *after* tomorrow."

"So, how long does it take you to get packed?"

"I don't know. I don't know what I'm going to need."

"Oh, yeah. Need." He moved back to pull open his front drawer. "You've got a passport. I know because I let you take two weeks vacation last year and you went to Paris. Paris! I don't know why article writers can't think of something original. What the hell can you write about Paris that hasn't been written a thousand times?"

"I went there on vacation. *Vacation.*"

"Nevertheless, a guy wanting to advance his career should plan his vacations with that in mind. Why didn't you go to Beirut?"

"I didn't want to get shot at."

"No guts. I don't know how you ever became a newspaperman. Never mind. This is an easy assignment. No danger at all. Even women go. They won't let you within a thousand yards of a lion and the giraffes and zebras won't let you within a thousand yards of *them.*"

"Thanks," I said. "Does that mean I can cancel my insurance?"

He ignored that. "Passport," he said. "You've got that. Visa. That usually takes a little time but, with the newspaper's influence with the Kenyan embassy, we've been able to do a hurry-up job. You can go there tomorrow and fill in the blanks. Take a photograph of yourself. A passport one will do, not that ten by twelve of you in front of that burning building with all the fire engines and medics around you, that you sneaked into the paper five years ago."

I said, "What are you doing for Kenya in payment, a front-page story on their president?"

"I don't think you really understand the newspaper game, James," he said. "Your airline tickets should be in tomorrow. There are some immunization shots you ought to take—cholera, yellow fever, but they take a while to become effective. Besides, you probably took them when you went to Paris. If we have to provide written proof, we can forge something. I know some people."

"Where do you think I stayed in Paris? In the sewers?"

He picked up the Bird Watcher's paper again. "You're going to be at Iberia Airlines on Thursday at five o'clock. Got it? Break all your dates for the next two weeks. Tell the girls you'll bring them back some powdered rhinoceros horn." He shuffled through related papers and handed me one. "Here's suggested clothing. Dress warmly and bring a hot water bottle. Kenya's on the equator, but it's seven thousand feet high and there's snow in the mountains. The flowers freeze at night. Oh, yes, and take binoculars and a telescopic camera. If your article is any good, we might run some pictures of animals. See if you can get a lion eating a zebra. Well, eating anything. And elephants. Everybody loves elephants. It'll give your article class."

I looked at the sheet. "This says the deadline for signing up is March twenty-first. Don't you think you're a little late on this?"

"Oh, that," he waved. "Don't worry about it. We got your application in in plenty of time. You're accepted."

"Oh, that?" I said. "You've been sitting on this all this time?"

"Sure. You know we have to plan the travel section well in advance."

"Why didn't you plan *me* well in advance?"

"Hell," he said, "we didn't know what we'd be assigning you to do where. If we had something else on deck for you, we'd get somebody else. Driscoll or Merryweather." He gave me his beaming "you're our number-one man" grin. "Had to keep the options open. It's only a matter of whose name we put on the dotted line." He half rose from his chair, the "number-one man" grin still on his face. "You're the one we wanted, James. And I'm happy as hell that you're going to be the one to do it!"

He knew, of course, I didn't want to play second fiddle to Driscoll or Merryweather. He knew he could make me go. That was the galling part. It sounded great. I liked the idea. A safari in Africa would have been my next vacation. But he could have told me. Except he didn't want me relishing the assignment. He wanted it to be a *job*.

TWO

CHECK-IN TIME at Iberia Airlines was 5:00 P.M. on June nineteenth, so said the ticket packet Bill Clayborn handed me. I dutifully arrived at the check-in desk promptly at five on the nineteenth and encountered the Bird Watchers Society African Safari tour director, a tall, thirtyish man with curly brown hair and mustache, wearing a webbed plastic New York Yankees baseball cap. His name was Busby Morgan and he was by the weigh-in desk holding a sheaf of papers and a pen to check names, and he was apologetic for not being able to get us group seating on the plane.

I was third to arrive, he said, and had I brought passport, visa, and all the recommended paraphernalia? I said I'd brought everything but the cat and heaved my heavy bag onto the scales.

That bag was loaded with warm clothing, cool clothing, a couple of cheap cotton safari shirts made in India, two pairs of slacks, two sweaters, one light, one heavy. I had a wool jacket, a visored cap (Kenya is on the equator, the guide list reminded us, and the sun beats straight down with a heavy beam—never mind the temperature, beware the sun), one 35 mm Nikon with all the attachments, filters, telephoto lens, electronic flash (hippos, so I understood, only come out of the water at night). And binoculars. I have a very fine pair, given me when I started my reporting career by a very lovely young lady who is now only a remote part of my life. (She's married and lives in Brazil and sends

Christmas cards with the printed message, "Holiday
Greetings from Richard, Pam, Sara, Jimmy, dog Spot and
cat Timmy.")

There was the shaving kit, the necessary changes of socks
and underwear, a pair of sneakers for light going, water-
proof shoes for slogging, decent shoes for show. Also for
show was a proper jacket, three ties, and a pair of carefully
folded pants. Reading material, notebooks, and on-board
incidentals, including a flask of rye, were in my briefcase,
gift from another lovely lady of my past who no longer
writes.

Check-in time was 5:00, but take-off time was 7:00. Airlines like to have the troops report early. Their attitude toward passengers is that of doctors toward patients. Keep 'em
waiting. Instead of old magazines, though, airports solace
passengers with gift shops, restaurants, and liquor stores.
What gold mines *they* are! No wonder we wait. Plane
schedules are probably concocted by airport barkeeps.

I gave two Manhattans' worth of business to one of the
barkeeps, took a small table by myself, and, for the first
time, paid serious attention to the packet of trip material.
My flight ticket booked me to Nairobi, but there was a day's
stopover in Madrid. We wouldn't get to Nairobi till Saturday and out to the game parks till Sunday. The safari was
limited to twenty people, but only nineteen were listed. *My*
latecomer name wasn't included.

There was a couple named Kirby from Stamford, a couple named Baldwin from Rowayton, a man named Sidney
Leggett from Westport, a Colonel and Roxanne Dagger
from New York City. Of those seven, the colonel was the
only member whose first name wasn't listed and, unlike the
other couples, he and Roxanne had different home addresses. His was the Philosophers Club on Vanderbilt
Avenue, a diehard-male-only private club which is

excruciatingly difficult to join, and Roxanne's was 301 East Fifty-seventh Street, site of one of those posh high-rise apartment buildings that have been springing up like toadstools all over Manhattan's East Side the past twenty years, and are now infiltrating the West.

The other twelve names had no home addresses, just the legend, "The Cartwright Company." Three of the twelve were, themselves, named Cartwright: Phineas, Richard, and Samantha. I took it that the Cartwright Company was underwriting a safari tour for nine of its employees, with two of the company heads and one wife going along for the ride.

WHEN I WAS THROUGH with my two Manhattans, I found my way to the VIP room Iberia had set aside for the tour group. It was a middle-sized space containing four rows of twenty seats each, another row against the back wall, and a gathering area at the front. Busby Morgan was already there with a wiry, gray, eighty-year-old man whom he introduced as Sidney Leggett.

"Sid here has a life-list of five hundred and forty-three," Busby told me as Leggett and I shook hands.

"And you've guaranteed to add me a hundred," Leggett cackled, punching Morgan's arm.

Morgan pooh-poohed him. "I only guarantee *fifty*. The rest is up to you."

I felt it was my turn, so I said, "What's a life-list?"

Leggett stared dumbfounded. Busby, after assessing that I wasn't pulling his leg, tried to put me at ease by explaining, "It's a list of different species of birds one has *personally* seen and identified. Sid hasn't been to Africa before. He's got one of the longest life-lists in the world and he wants to expand it. He wants to be numero uno!"

Leggett was cackling at me querulously, "You're going on a bird watching expedition and you don't know what a life-list is?"

I pleaded ignorance. "My boss told me it was 'animal watching.' You mean all we're going to see are birds?"

"Oh," Leggett assured me, "there'll be animals. You can hardly watch a red or yellow-billed oxpecker picking ticks out of a giraffe's hide without seeing the giraffe!"

With that dismissal, he directed his bird talk to Busby. I took a seat against the wall, pulled out my notebook, and did jottings for my article.

A couple came in, plump, middle-aged, and beaming. They greeted both Morgan and Leggett familiarly, paying no attention to me. I put them down as bird watchers: either the Kirbys or the Baldwins.

Two minutes after them, a lone man came in. He was tall, six three or four, stately, with a lean face, a thick thatch of gray hair, and a gray mustache. His eyes were gray, too, and they were intriguing. Even from a distance, they suggested great depths, but they said absolutely nothing. More than that, though they looked nowhere in particular, they missed nothing. His glance passed over me like a flashlight beam and did not come my way again, yet I felt read, catalogued, and dismissed. It was not kind to my ego and made me wish I'd attracted more of his attention.

His other qualities, which I noted down, included: 1) An erect, military bearing. 2) A slight weakness in his left leg, a weakness he made every effort to conceal and which, thus, made me pleased to suspect. 3) He carried with him a mag-nificent cane. It was ebony black, trim but thick, and the head of it had to be solid gold. By the weight of it, it couldn't be anything else. It was a massive head, shaped like the grip of a gun, and the newcomer wielded and handled the cane, not as an aid to walking, for it only casually touched the ground, but as if it were an extension of himself. It was an awesome but unconscious part of his personality.

Of course he had to be Colonel Dagger. He even went with the name. Except—there was supposed to be a Roxanne Dagger with him and he'd come alone.

Well, why not? They had different addresses. They didn't have to have come together. They didn't even have to be related. But it left me with the question. Who was Roxanne? A wife? An ex-wife? A relative? A coincidence?

The new man met and chatted with the others. He smiled, seemed friendly, talkative, even gregarious and, despite that cane, not the least bit dangerous. But there was always that reserve, and the blank eyes. He listened more than he talked, and I got the impression he heard more than was said, sensed more than he saw. Though his eyes did not come my way again, I had the feeling he knew exactly where I was and what I was doing. He knew where everybody was. He knew everything that was going on.

A new couple came in, the man plump, with thin reddish hair, a grin, and a cardboard safari helmet, the woman gray, with glasses, and breezy. The colonel's eyes flickered, not really in their direction, which was nearly behind, but enough to show he had absorbed their arrival.

As I EXPECTED, the Cartwright contingent arrived en masse, most of them buzzing and giggling and tumbling all over each other like kids with a new computer game. All except for the three members of the Cartwright family itself, who were as easy to spot as an oil rig in the Sahara. They were linked together, they looked as if they were swallowing cod-liver oil, and they were *avoided*. Old Phineas (he called the younger man "Richard") looked as if he hadn't laughed since the *Titanic* sank and nothing about this ven-

ture would produce a like response. He was gray and glow-
ery and made me glad I didn't work for the Cartwright
Company.

The son, Richard, looked like a fifty-year-old version of
the father. He had the same thatch of gray hair, except his
was thinning at the back, and he was a little plumper, the
peek of a paunch showing over his belt, but not enough to
get into jogging clothes about. Unlike his father, who had
an earthy quality to him, Richard wore the haughty air of
the privileged. The old man bore the tight, suspicious scowl
of the moneymaker. Richard enjoyed the lackluster disdain
of the money-spender. They did not look at each other, but
when Phineas muttered, Richard turned an instant ear.

Samantha, Richard's wife, was a bit something else. I
guessed her ten years Richard's junior, but eons different
otherwise. She had the tanned and weathered face of an
outdoorswoman and the figure of an athlete. Richard was
pale and puffy and looked as if his acquaintance with the
outdoors was sipping a gin and tonic on the patio. Her body
was trim and wiry, not soft and buxom; an attractive figure
but not a sexy one.

She wasn't the most alluring beauty of the Cartwright
group—I'd give that palm to Harriet Gamble, when I get to
her—but Samantha *did* have flair. Harriet couldn't touch
her in that. Samantha's hair was dark, with a streak of gray,
she had a Thoroughbred's features, with only a few crow's-
feet around the eyes, and she dressed her erect, slim, trim
figure in designer clothes, which she wore as if she'd been
born in them. Harriet had designers, too, but she couldn't
carry it off as well. She'd only *married* into them.

The other women came from Plainsville.

ENOUGH NOTE-TAKING. I was writing a travel article and needed hard evidence. Time to get out of my seat and start mingling.

An article-writer, wanting proper information, doesn't, of course, tell his subjects he's writing an article. That's not the way to acquire unbiased views. So I tucked my notebook in my pocket, presented myself as a vacationer, and tried to meet and learn as much about the other members of the safari tour as I could before flight time.

The one I most wanted to pump for information was the "Mysterious Colonel Dagger," who had 1) no first name, 2) a gold cane, and 3) a no-show companion named Roxanne.

But, as if he'd read my mind, the colonel had withdrawn to a secluded corner, fenced himself into a "private" territory, and was reading a book. So I only got to meet the rest of the group; the bird watchers and the Cartwright contingent, which, I learned, consisted of nine merit-winning employees, the African safari being their reward, plus, of course, the already identified company owner, his son, and daughter-in-law.

The nine others, so I noted down as soon as I could, included two married couples, two single women, and three single men, and I had them all identified and their names memorized within the next twenty minutes, after which I retired to the privacy of the men's room to write it all down. Here's what I got:

Going on this trip (I'm guessing at their ages):

1. Busby Morgan, thirtyish (tour guide, tall, young, mustache, Yankee baseball cap)
2. James Addison, 35 (myself, of course)
3. Colonel Dagger, mid-fifties (tall, gray, secretive— not even a first name! Golden cane)

4. Roxanne Dagger (no show)
5. Sidney Leggett (eighty-year-old bird watcher. Life-list of 543)
6. Harry Baldwin, 55(?) (bird watcher, plump, reddish hair, grins, cardboard safari hat)
7. Mary Ellen Baldwin, 50(?) (bird watcher, wife of Harry, gray, glasses, breezy)
8-9. Jerry and June Kirby, 45(?) (bird watchers)

Then there were the Cartwright people:

1. Phineas Cartwright, 75 (head of firm, gray, suspicious, feared and disliked)
2. Richard Cartwright, 50 (son of Phineas, arrogant, indoorsy, feared and disliked)
3. Samantha Cartwright, 40 (wife of Richard, athletic, outdoorsy, reasonably attractive)
4. George Gamble, 45 (head of Cartwright's legal department, puffy, squirrellike cheeks)
5. Harriet Gamble, 35 (wife of George. Attractive and knows it)
6. Marshall Benedict, 60-65 (one of the high-ups in the company. Large man, expansive manner)
7. Sylvia Benedict, 60 (Marshall's wife. Small. Wrenlike)
8. Lucy Children, fiftyish (personal secretary to Phineas. Large, gray, shapeless, dedicated)
9. Jennifer Long, thirtyish (bookkeeper, thin, pale, glasses—no personality)
10. Duncan Hawley, 55 (head of production—company makes ball bearings, uncombed, relaxed. Alcoholic?)
11. Peter Tower, 35 (salesman. Bright, aggressive, good-looking)

12. Neville Street, 35 (salesman. Good-looking, smart, and ambitious) (Street and Tower tied for salesman of the year.)

Those were the people I'd be spending the next two weeks with—and maybe a Roxanne Dagger, if she showed.

THREE

Thursday, June 19

ROXANNE DAGGER *did* show, and I should have *known* she'd be the colonel's daughter, not his wife.

Only a daughter would have had a different address. Only a daughter would have come bounding in with five minutes to spare, and only a daughter would have found her father looking at his watch, wondering if she'd make it on time.

She had made it, however, and she lighted up that drab room and that drab company like a fairy godmother turning a pumpkin into a coach. She was in her late twenties, with a tossed mane of dark hair, wearing a tan blouse and safari skirt. Her figure was alluring, her posture athletic, her manner graceful and energetic, and her face, with its dark brows accenting blue-gray eyes, beguiling. Forget the other women in the group. Forget all the other women at the airport. She alone could have launched a thousand ships.

Those lustrous blue-gray eyes were only for Dad, though, as she crossed the room to get to him, there by the windows, and stand on tiptoe to give him a big buss on the cheek, a kiss he endured with the air of someone resigned to the idea that females can't control their emotions. Secretly, though, I think he was pleased. It gave him a cachet to be the object of the affections of the most wondrous female within a ten-mile radius.

You should have seen her effect on all the men at hand—not just me. Every husband looked up at her arrival, gaped, then glanced to see where his wife was before he stared again. The two young Cartwright single men, Peter Tower and Neville Street, took a spontaneous synchronized half step in her direction, and paused to adjust their ties. Their automatic, all-too-predictable reaction warned me on the instant I was in for a lot of competition persuading her I was the most eligible male she'd encountered over the next fortnight.

Right then, though, the three of us were on hold. She didn't yet know we existed. When her father had entered the room, he saw *everybody*. When she entered, she saw *nobody*. I'd rather have had it the other way around.

But now she was with Papa, holding his arm, looking after him like a seeing-eye dog. He plainly didn't need that kind of care, but women are nurturers whether it's needed or not. She went through his ticket folder with him to see where he sat, then opened her straw purse to compare it with her own folder. Busby Morgan approached to confirm her identity and check off her name. Immediately, Neville Street was at Busby's side, horning in, getting an introduction. I looked over at the outmaneuvered Peter Tower. He pretended he hadn't been competing, but he was chafing.

The 747 didn't take off until half past eight and it was so packed I was surprised it could get off the ground. As Busby had warned, our group was scattered among the other passengers like seeds in the wind and I only had two contacts with any of the others in the group the whole flight.

The first was when the meal was served and old Phineas Cartwright stood up and bellowed that the airline was trying to poison him! He stalked past me down the aisle heading for the lavatory, red-faced, choking, threatening vengeance, and waving away help, while a flutter of nervous stewardesses followed in his wake. When he emerged, five minutes later, the expression on his face boded ill for the flight attendants, the airline, and the food suppliers who had conspired to do him in.

The second was shortly before midnight when, bored by the movie, I toured the darkened plane to stretch my legs. Old Phineas, recovering from his "poisoning," was smack in front of the screen, watching the action like a seven-year-old at a Saturday afternoon western, soothing his stomach with bags of airline peanuts.

Farther ahead, outside the midplane lavatories, I overheard two men, conversing in low tones, mention Cartwright's name, and I paused to eavesdrop. At the time, I thought the information might help my article.

"He's gonna ruin it for everybody," the first one muttered darkly. "He's starting already. I *tried* to get him to stay home."

The other replied, "Isn't it better he's *here*? Otherwise, wouldn't you be afraid there'd be a new man at your desk when you got back?"

"Not I," said the first. "He knows better. Both of them do. Lucy's the one who has to worry. She doesn't know it, but this is her swan song, her reward for long years of service."

"The hell you say," answered the other. "The old man can't get along without her."

"He can't, but Richard can. I don't give the old man six more months, no matter what he says, and when Richard comes in, nothing belonging to the old man's gonna stay."

"Oh, God," the other groaned. "There goes my job. Richard hates me."

One of the lavatory doors opened and the conversation stopped. I moved to the corner to catch a glimpse of the two men who were talking. It was just in time to see George Gamble, the lawyer with the squirrel cheeks, the one who was worried about his job, step inside the cramped lavatory space and shut the door. The other, who moved back to let the departing passenger by, was the slouchy, slack, graying Duncan Hawley, head of production. He lounged against the bulkhead and lighted a cigarette. The smoking section was aft, but he didn't care.

Neither of them saw me and I circled back to keep it that way.

WE LANDED in Madrid in bright sunshine at 2:30 in the morning New York time, but 8:30 their time, and, after showing our passports, the tour group collected around Busby Morgan at a Holcomb Travel Agency sign and buses took us to a nearby hotel to wait for the midnight flight to Nairobi.

We were a bedraggled group. Most hadn't slept, but a few of us held firm and went into town to the Museo del Prado, Madrid's fabled museum. I'd been there before, but didn't mind going again and it was a chance to get better acquainted with some of the group. You can't amass too much material if you're doing an article.

I shared a taxi with Marshall and Sylvia Benedict and said I'd come to Africa to see the animals, that I thought it would be a fun vacation.

Both Benedicts were alert and interested and felt the same way. "Best idea George Gamble ever had," Marshall said when we started out. "About time old Phineas unlocked his purse and gave his people some of what they deserve."

"This is not a yearly event then?" I ventured.

Marshall Benedict shook his head. He was a large man, as large and as expansive as his wife was petite and birdlike. She could have been a female wren, dowdy, quiet, in a plain brown dress to match her plain brown hair. She had a narrow, pointed nose and patrician features, but she sat tightly in a corner of the backseat, her husband filling the

rest of it, while I rode with the driver. Marshall had a florid
face, a thick head of white hair and black bushy eyebrows.
Everything about him was gross and overgrown, like a giant
puppy dog.

"Naw," Marshall replied with a broad wave of the hand.
"You wouldn't find old Phineas thinking up something like
this on his own. His idea was loving cups. It's always loving
cups. George was the one who argued for a trip. He got
everybody so excited about the idea the old man *had* to go
along with it. I took a poll. Two weeks in Africa, to one
week in Acapulco, or one week in Rio. I was betting on Rio,
but George did the safari last year and xeroxed a report that
sold a majority on Africa. Of course we get an extra week
on this trip and that helped George sell it. He's been dying
to come back."

"He must carry a lot of weight with Phineas."

"Naw," Marshall said again. "He carried weight with the
staff. Phineas doesn't believe in spending the money. This
is a first, and I know because I've been with the company
longer than anyone else except the old man. I taught Richard everything he knows. That's Richard riding in the other
cab behind us. Gray-haired guy, looks like his father—has
the tanned, dark-haired wife."

"I know him," I said. "His wife isn't coming into town
with him?"

"She's going to bed. Richard says she didn't sleep on the
plane. I dropped off the moment the movie came on. Never
knew a thing till breakfast." He patted his wife's knee with
a hand that engulfed it. "Sylvie here, she slept, too. Didn't
you, Sylvie?"

Sylvia shook her head. "Really, I couldn't sleep a wink.
That horrible movie kept me awake."

He turned to her solicitously. "What're you coming in to
the museum for? Why don't *you* go to bed?"

She half laughed. "And miss this? This's the first vacation you've ever taken. I can sleep when you're back at work."

"Now look," he complained, "you know I can't take vacations. I've got to know how to run the company. The number three man has to know as much as *numero uno* and *numero dos*. Especially when *numero dos* is Richard."

Sylvie looked out the window and I thought there was a tear in her eye. "What," I asked Marshall, to bridge the moment, "caused old Mr. Cartwright to kick up such a fuss on the plane?"

"Pay no attention," Marshall answered with another broad wave of the hand. "Phineas wants to be the big cheese, attract everybody's notice. Success has spoiled him rotten. Everybody's got to 'yes' him to death. Anybody who doesn't had better look for other employment. I'd hate to be in Lucy Children's shoes." He sighed at the thought. "She's stayed with the company so long because she's the only one who can handle him—put up with his quirks and whims. I don't know how she does it, and I don't know *why* she does it. I'd've hopped the first freight to China if it'd been me. As it is, I have to bite my tongue every time I go into his office. No wonder I've got ulcers." He pressed a big hand against his side to produce some pain, then clapped Sylvie on the knee again with his enormous hand. "Eh, sweetie?" It brought her some of the pain as well, for she winced.

She was used to his manhandling, however, and followed with a nod. "But it won't be for much longer. He's stepping down very soon now."

"Don't you believe it," Marshall answered. "He's been saying that for five years. It makes everybody's eyes glow. That's why he does it. He's *never* going to step down. He can't stand the thought of Richard taking over."

I said, "Do you *want* him to step down? Do you believe life would be better under Richard?"

"Ugh" was Marshall's response. "That'd be like tossing a coin with no heads. They're both different. It's a question which one's worse. They're worse in different ways."

"If Richard takes over," mouselike Sylvia Benedict said softly, and patted her husband's knee, "Marshall will retire."

"Fat chance," Marshall answered. "I'll have to stay on to keep the company afloat."

"Richard will fire you," Sylvia said with quiet conviction. "He's jealous because you know more than he does. It would be better if you retired."

"Richard couldn't afford to fire me," Marshall retorted. "Like I say, the company would sink."

"And Richard would rather let it sink than have *you* save it."

FOUR

THE PRADO held our attention until half past twelve. We saw ghoulish Bosch paintings on the second floor, rooms and rooms of Goyas, including both the naked and the quickly painted "clothed" Maja, and rooms of Raphaels, and then we'd had it. Sylvie and I were dragging and Marshall was getting bored. He said he liked baseball.

A cab took us back to the hotel in time for lunch, and I sacked out for the rest of the afternoon. Sidney Leggett was sharing the room with me but I never saw him. He was off with camera and binoculars seeing if Madrid could enhance his life-list.

I came down for dinner at ten after eight, found the dining hall didn't open till half past, and cruised into the cocktail lounge. It was a dim room, with a crowded bar and not so crowded tables. At one of the farthest tables, Peter Tower and Neville Street huddled around a smiling and beguiling Roxanne Dagger. They hovered so close she couldn't put a hand to her hair without backing them off. Her smiles and pleasantries seemed evenly distributed and I couldn't tell which one of the two was ahead.

I assumed, since Roxanne was so occupied, that her father wasn't around but, to my surprise, there he was, alone at a tiny table against the wall, holding and occasionally sipping from a light Scotch and soda, paying no attention to his daughter. Our eyes met for the first time and he nodded me over. Until now, he hadn't acknowledged my existence and I almost wanted to look around to see if he meant somebody else.

I approached, he smiled, and his eyes didn't seem quite as opaque. I thought I detected twinkles of humor deep down inside, down where a man can laugh at the world, but *deep*, where the laugh is bitter.

"Would you join me for a drink, Mr. Addison?" he said, and indicated the facing chair.

So he knew my name? It shouldn't have been too hard to figure out, but he said it just as I was starting to hold out my hand and introduce myself.

"Yes, thank you, *Colonel*." That would let him know I'd figured out his.

I sat down and he summoned one of the red-jacketed waiters. "What's your choice?"

"The same as yours would be fine. That *is* Scotch and soda?"

"Thin Scotch and soda. Very thin. I daresay you'd like something a little more vigorous." He was appraising me and nodded, as if certain. Then he said, "How's the article coming?"

That made me jump. "Article?"

He grimaced apologetically. "I *am* moving too fast. The trip's hardly begun. You can't even have started to shape it. You're still in the information-collection stage."

I was half off my chair wanting to demand how the hell he knew about my article. That was my *secret*. But just then the waiter came and Colonel Dagger gave him my order and when the waiter had turned and gone, the colonel was on a different tack. "Mr. Addison," he said, "I don't mean to be inquisitive, but have you signed up for a partner for this trip?"

"Partner?"

"They pair us in double rooms," he explained. "Are you paired with anybody?"

"I don't really know," I answered. "Right now I'm sharing a room with Sidney Leggett. I don't know who arranged it."

"If you aren't committed to Mr. Leggett," the colonel went on, "I'm in need of a partner, and if you should be free—"

You won't believe how flattered I felt. The aloof and distant colonel had noticed *me*. And there was no overlooking the fact it might give me an advantage over Peter Tower and Neville Street with the colonel's beautiful daughter!

"Sir," I said, hiding just how joyful I was, "I'd be delighted."

"Mr. Leggett won't mind?"

"Hardly. I never saw him before yesterday afternoon. He fancies birds. I do not. We have nothing in common."

The colonel's expression hinted relief. "You ease my mind," he said. "I have to explain. I'm traveling, as you have noted, with a daughter. She is, of course, a generation younger than I and she holds the *modern* view that it's perfectly all right for a father and daughter to share a hotel room together. I'm from the more old-fashioned school that feels such an arrangement is not in the best of taste. That's why I approached you."

"Perfectly natural," I said as the waiter served my Scotch and soda. Actually, I couldn't see anything wrong with *her* arrangement, but I was pleased to be involved in the problem. Peter Tower and Neville Street, hunched over the delightful and delicious Roxanne, didn't know what was coming up on their blind side.

"I have faults," he warned me, lifting and staring through his half-finished drink. "Sometimes I'm restless at night. If you wake and find me prowling about, pay no attention. If

I should disturb you in my sleep, shake me and wake me. It
would be a favor to us both.''

"Sir," I said, "you won't disturb me. I can sleep through
anything.'' I reflected. "Except the movie on the plane last
night. *That* couldn't put me to sleep.''

HE WAS GONE THEN, to make arrangements with Busby
Morgan. Peter, Neville, and Roxanne departed at the same
time, but in a different direction, and I was left with my
Scotch and soda, which I took in with me to dinner.

I was late to the meal and the only unoccupied seat was at
Phineas's, Richard's, and Samantha's table. There was a
space for a fourth and I realized, when I looked around with
despairing glance, it was the only space open for me.

I smiled at the three Cartwrights and they smiled back.
Even the old man smiled. There was an unhappy distaste in
his at bottom, but it could be defined, if you give Webster
leeway, as a smile.

My presence did seem to animate the trio, as if there was
now cause for conversation. But I couldn't help evaluating
them at close range. Phineas, his white, stringy hair over-
long, as if he resented the high price of haircuts, had a sal-
low face with heavy creases down his cheeks, and heavier
ones at the ends of his lips, like weights pulling down the
corners of his mouth. And there were those hostile, suspicious, avaricious eyes, "dollar-sign eyes," the eyes of a
money-grabber. The eyes of a killer.

Richard was dangerous, too, but in another way. He had
an arrogant look, the disdain of eye, the upward lift of chin
that people acquire when they try to look down on other
people and aren't quite tall enough. But threaten him? Try
to dispossess him? His father was brutal. Richard was sin-
ister.

And there was Samantha, a wiry female, lean and muscular, weathered and tanned, a good deal older than she looked. The wrinkles around her eyes suggested forty years of creasing, but her body would have done well by a twenty-five-year-old. Perhaps not quite. It was lean and hard, flat and trim. It was the body of a woman who *stayed* in shape, rather than the body of one who hadn't yet discovered what it was to *lose* her shape. To look at her and Richard sitting together, you wouldn't want to make bets as to who could out-arm-wrestle whom. Then there were her eyes, the windows to her soul. The windows told me she was a bitter, frustrated, unhappy woman who hated the men she was with.

Swift, green-jacketed waiters served the meal, and service was rapid, except at our table. Phineas would have none of the provided meal, ordered a menu, and insisted on pointing his finger at every item, requiring that it be explained.

"Sir, the English is down this side."

"I know where the English is. I *talk* the damned language. I want to know what does *this* mean?"

Samantha hemmed and hawed, studying her husband and father-in-law more than she did her own menu. What she finally ordered was a "cheapie," as if she were the maid being treated to lunch because there was nothing in the refrigerator.

Richard went the other way, pointing to the most expensive dishes offered. "I'll have *that*!" he exclaimed, and on down the page, ordering à la carte, his eyes never leaving the side of the menu which listed the prices. He didn't know what he was ordering, only the cost. Phineas, who chose and only picked at a small salad, was obviously hosting the occasion.

I tried to make conversation by noting the anticipation of the group for the forthcoming trip. I supposed Phineas and Richard must be pleased with George Gamble for coming up with the idea.

At that remark, Richard pretended to cool his soup. Phineas didn't pretend anything. "Gamble," he said, "thought this suggestion would put him in good with me." He gave his son a skull-like grin that would have scared the wits out of a teenage horror-show freak. "Gamble," he announced to us all, "thought he had more influence in this company than he had. He somehow thought he could get us to do his bidding."

The frightening smile came again. "Gamble doesn't know it—not yet—but when we get back home, he's not going to have a home. He's going to be *gone*."

I tried again, uneasily, and remarked about the pleasure of seeing wild animals in one of the last places they existed. Phineas made a face. "If you can't shoot 'em or eat 'em, what good are they?"

"I suppose they're good to look at."

"Sonny," he said to me, "I got three rooms full of paintings in my house. They're good to look at, too, but they're increasing in value all the time. Those animals aren't doing anything but eating food cattle could be grazing on. What's the profit in that?"

"They build up Kenya's tourist trade."

"Ha," Phineas snorted. "The park we're going to would bring in a lot more money if the Kenyan government got rid of the animals and put up houses. If you want to maximize the value of real estate, *build* on it."

Samantha said, "Phineas believes in building skyscrapers on golf courses."

"Golf," he told her, "is for people like you—women who have husbands out making money for them to spend. You don't see *Richard* playing golf."

Richard said, "You don't give me the chance."

"You couldn't play if you tried," his father sneered. "In twenty years you can't even run the company."

"How do you know? You haven't let me try."

Phineas pointed a finger. "That's because I'm smart."

I said to Samantha, "You're a golfer?"

She nodded emphatically. "And damned good. Never mind what these old men say. I have more golfing trophies on my mantel than Phineas has pictures in his art collection."

"But," Phineas reminded her, "they aren't increasing in value. They're only collecting dust."

RICHARD AND SAMANTHA had had enough of the old man and skipped dessert. When they rose, I did, too, but Phineas waved me down with the kind of peremptory gesture he used with his staff. I was tempted to ignore it, but he had something to tell me, and my curiosity was too strong. I bid Richard and Samantha good night and resumed my seat.

"Well," the old man said when we were alone. "What do you think of them?"

"Your son and daughter-in-law?"

"Who else? What do you think of my son?" His voice turned into a sneer. "A man who wears a watch on both wrists, a digital on his left wrist, and one with hands on the right? I say, 'He needs all the help he can get.' What do you say?"

"I'm sorry," I answered. "I didn't notice the two watches. How does *he* explain it?"

"He claims the digital is his tried and true, the one on his right wrist is an award, a prize. It's chrome. It can't be worth more than a hundred dollars. Some prize!"

"What'd he win it for?"

"He won't say." Phineas sneered in contempt. "If that's a prize, I'm the queen of England. What would *he* ever win a prize for? He didn't learn how to tie his shoes until he was in the fourth grade." He dismissed his son with a wave of the hand. "Enough about him. How do you read *her*? Tell me what you think of Samantha."

"Sir, I don't know. What do you want me to say?"

Phineas brushed back his stringy locks and gave me a smile such as would become the face of a dying man. "She's a parasite," he said. "*Who* can't see it? She *lives* on the golf course, practicing putting, driving, whatever golfers do. She does it all. You call her at home and she's never home." He took a breath and held it, swelling in size until his face became red. "I had a wife once," he went on. "She played the *same* game as Samantha, and I don't mean golf. She wanted to wear mink, eat chocolates, and ride in a Rolls Royce, all at *my* expense. You know where she is *now*?"

"No," I said.

"Scrubbing floors." He gave me his death's-head grin again. "In a nunnery." He stared at me with his evil eyes to make sure I understood. "She owes what she is to them!"

"Not to you?"

Phineas swelled again. "Not by *me*. Nothing she has or is, is by *me*!"

He was proud. He was the proudest man I ever saw.

It was quarter of ten and we were alone in the dining room. I pushed aside my dessert, said I had to pack, and went back to my room.

IN THE HALL OUTSIDE, Roxanne Dagger was waiting.

FIVE

"WELL, HEL-LO," I said, masking my surprise. God, she was a lovely-looking creature, and she *was* waiting for me?

"Mr. Addison," she answered, distress evident in her face, and she came so close I thought she was going to put a beseeching hand on my arm.

"The name is Jim," I corrected. "And you're Roxanne, not Miss Dagger, or Ms., or however you address yourself." I aimed my key for the door. "And do come in."

She shook her head. "No, please, Mr. Addison," she said, refusing the intimacy of the name "Jim." "I only came to ask a favor. I'll only be a minute."

"Favor?" I asked, and was ready to bow and say, "Anything, dear lady."

But she fortunately spoke first. "Yes. My father's talked to you about rooming together." Her eyes became appealing. "Would you reconsider his proposal?"

That befuddled me. "You mean you don't want me to room with him?"

She gave a nod and went on quickly. "It's not because you're doing an article and I'm afraid you'll—" She hesitated. "I don't mean he might appear belittled—"

That I was writing an article was supposed to be my best-kept secret. "Writing an article?" I said, smarting. "What do you have, a pipeline to the newspaper guild?"

She sensed my anger. "Oh, no, sir. That's only what my father told me. Maybe he was wrong?"

"This is all nonsense," I said. "What would my writing or not writing articles have to do with rooming with your father?"

Roxanne became appealing again. Once more she almost put her hand on my sleeve and I couldn't but note the long slender fingers, the shaped nails, their tint matching the light red of her lipstick. "It has nothing to do with who you are, or *what* you are," she assured me, "whether you write articles or sell Mickey Mouse watches. I'm only worried about—" She hesitated and finalized, "—you."

(Forget the "you." She meant her father.)

"Thanks for the thought," I said. "What're you worried about?"

"Please understand me," she said. "You don't know what you're doing."

"You mean because he doesn't sleep well at night? He's told me that. I don't really think he'll keep me awake."

"It's not that," she said. "He's ill. He needs someone to take care of him."

"Ill? He seems perfectly fit to me."

"That's because you don't know him," she went on urgently. "He needs someone to look after him."

"Despite the excuse he gave me, I think the reason is, he doesn't want *anybody* to look after him."

Now she implored me. "He doesn't want to give in. Don't you see?"

I shook my head. Never mind the pretty lady. The colonel had made a request and I'd agreed to it. I couldn't go back on my word. If she had medical evidence that he was a kook, then I might have to listen.

"What's wrong with him?" I asked. "How is he ill? I mean, should he have a doctor?"

She couldn't produce medical evidence, only assurances. "No, nothing like that. It's nothing a doctor can treat. His ailments go too deep."

"Including not wanting you to help him?"

Her mouth tightened. "You disbelieve me? In the first place, he *drinks*. I mean, like nobody you ever *saw*. He's an alcoholic!"

She paused as if that was supposed to send me flying.

But I'd written an article on alcoholism and I'd shared a drink with Colonel Dagger this afternoon. If he really were an alcoholic, he'd be in the gutter by now. The old saw is true: with an alcoholic, one drink is *too* many, a *hundred* too few.

"Where is he?" I asked.

"In the room, napping. He's afraid he won't sleep on the plane tonight."

"Is he dead drunk?"

"Of course not." Roxanne was impatient. "But that doesn't mean he isn't an alcoholic. He just won't admit it."

"But he doesn't get drunk?"

She shook her head in wonder. "I've never seen him drunk. I've seen him drink. God, can he drink! He got that from his second wife. That's when I first met him. I mean— when he and my mother split, I went with her, and I didn't even know he was alive until I was twenty. Now he's just gone through a *third* divorce!" Her eyes beseeched me for understanding, and this time she actually did put her hand on my sleeve. "Can you imagine what it must be like for a man to go through *three* divorces?"

"No, I can't," I confessed. "I haven't even been married. But, can you? You're not only not married, you're not a man, either."

"That doesn't matter," she insisted. "I *know* my father. He's sensitive. He *feels* things."

I said, "I have a friend who got divorced after twenty-nine years." I put a covering hand on hers. "And I have never seen, in all my life, a happier man!" I patted the slender, beautiful hand upon my sleeve. "How do you know your father is miserable about the divorce?"

"Because he won't discuss it with me."

"And you want him to?"

"It would give him peace. No man, Mr. Addison, is an island. We must share or we *die*. You're a writer. You should understand that."

"I'm a writer, and I can't even understand why you won't call me 'Jim.'"

"All right, damn it, 'Jim.' You ought to be able to understand it, but you don't, and it doesn't matter *what* your name is."

"I understand, very well, people who don't want to communicate. I'm one myself."

"That's not so. People have to talk to other people. Even hermits talk to animals."

"It depends on whom you're talking to. I never shared anything with my parents. With my pals, yes. Sex, girls, God, *anything*. Not with my parents. There was a generation gap. I didn't believe they knew anything about such things." I patted her hand again. "And there's a generation gap between you and your father and maybe it's working in reverse. He doesn't think you can understand the things he could tell you."

Roxanne made a face and withdrew her hand. "Just what I'm afraid of," she said. "You're a *man*. You'll room with him and support him. You'll build his macho image. He needs a *woman*'s touch. He hides so much, and he needs to open doors." She gave me a deep look with her haunting blue eyes. "Do you know my father suffers pain?"

"No."

"Because he'd die rather than let you know! What do you think that cane is for? He wields it like a trophy, but it was given to fill a need." She looked at me despairingly. "He has bad dreams at night. He'll keep you awake with his dreams."

I said, "Why are you telling me this? Are you trying to get me to tell him I've changed my mind, that I don't want to room with him?"

Roxanne shook her head. "No," she confessed. "That wouldn't do. He wouldn't think well of you, and he'd be furious at me for trying to countermand his wishes."

"Well, then, what is it you want?"

Roxanne sighed and tears came in a rush to her eyes. "I suppose," she said, "what I want for him is tender loving care and he won't let me give it to him. He pretends he's so macho, and he hurts so much. He'd die before he'd let you know it, but *I* know it." She hesitated. "And, I guess, I'm selfish, too. I talked him into this trip with the idea that we'd be together, that we'd share something." She laughed a little. "I don't have a mother anymore, and I hardly know my father. As you can see, I have my own problems. Now I'm going to have to room alone, and I don't want to be alone."

All I could think of to say was, "I wish I could help. Do you want three in a room?"

That made her laugh. "My father thinks my rooming with *him* is bad enough. What would he think about my rooming with him and a handsome young man besides?"

"Thank you," I said, "for both the 'handsome' and the 'young.'"

"Ah, well," she said, with a smile that warmed me all the way to my toes, "I knew I wasn't going to change anything. My father dictates the terms of his own life, as well I know. Maybe all I wanted to do was get some gripes off my chest." She smiled in her special way again. "Thanks for listening."

Then she was gone.

SIX

NAIROBI WAS a seven hour and fifteen minute flight from Madrid and we arrived at 8:45 the next morning, which was 9:45 Nairobi time. Group headquarters for the night was the Nairobi Sabrina Hotel, where we registered and assembled in an adjacent meeting room for coffee and a briefing by a bouncy, gray-haired man named Gelston, who was the Nairobi representative of the Holcomb Travel Agency, host of our tour.

Four vans, Mr. Gelston told us, would transport our group on its safari, with five or six persons assigned to each van on a permanent basis. There would be a driver per van, and Busby Morgan, along with Lise Smith, a blond, middle-aged Dane he called forth and introduced, would take turns in various vans to tell us about the birds and animals we saw.

"You will leave here at eight tomorrow morning so I suggest you bring your luggage to the lobby when you come down for breakfast. That about covers everything except for any questions you might have. When you leave here, we have a bus waiting to take you to visit the baboon park before lunch for those of you who are interested. Other than that, your day here is free. You can explore Nairobi, shop, sleep, do what you want. One other program we have for your pleasure, besides the baboon park, is a slide show on birds, which Lise Smith will put on in this room at six." He spread his arms and beamed happily. "If those of you who wish to visit the baboon park will stay for a moment, the others may leave."

All remained except old Phineas Cartwright, who rose with a snort and pushed his way to the aisle. "Baboons!" he snapped. "I see enough of them every day at the plant."

Silence reigned until the old man had left the room, then came a collective sigh.

"It's *his* loss," Mr. Gelston advised us, commanding our attention again. "Now a few words of warning. For most of you, the baboons in this park will be your first experience with wild animals. They're used to people and not as suspicious and wary as the ones you'll see on safari, but don't forget, they are *still* wild animals. Though they're only half your size, you must remember they're much stronger than you are, much quicker, and they are equipped with ferocious teeth and powerful jaws. So, while they'll come up and take bread or rolls from your hand, don't try to pet them or touch them. And don't try to tease or antagonize them." He gave us his big smile again. "Another warning. Don't take anything valuable with you, and don't set anything down. They are arrant thieves and will grab anything they can get their hands on. And once they take off with something, you'll never see it again. One other thing. The baboons do expect to be fed, so if you want to see them close too, there are bread and rolls on hand in the kitchen for those who want them. The kitchen is over there; the bus is outside." He looked at his watch. "So shall we plan to meet at the bus in ten minutes?"

The bus was a jitney and was driven by a medium-sized, solidly built young Kenyan, born with the super-blackness only African natives inherit. Gelston introduced him as Amram Kitanyi, adding that, in Kenya, first names were heavily Biblical. During the five-minute drive to the park, Gelston addressed us in the aisle, enthusing about the privilege it was to have us here and what a wonderful time we'd have—how exciting we'd find it to see God's creatures in their native habitat.

Then we were through the park gates and disembarking in a small sandy parking area that opened onto roped paths leading through grassy spaces, past a pond, and near to trees. "Keep to the path," Mr. Gelston warned as we started off. "The rest of the park belongs to the baboons and they would resent anybody intruding on their territory."

The paths were being traveled by occasional wanderers and most baboons remained in the shade of the trees, watching while a few of their poorer fed fellows monitored the paths with outstretched paws. When our group, over twenty strong, started through, however, the waiting baboons bestirred themselves. All came loping over the grass and we were soon lined up along the guide ropes on both sides of the path handing out the chunks of bread and rolls we'd picked up on our foray through the Nairobi Sabrina Hotel's kitchen.

Dagger and I somehow had Roxanne to ourselves this trip. Maybe it was Dagger's cane. Maybe it was that Roxanne didn't stray. She watched me throw bread to the baboons and said they looked cute. Her father, on her other side, said they looked about as cute as a Hell's Angel putting on his motorcycle jacket. Roxanne wanted her father to give her a roll for the baboons. Her father said he hadn't brought any; let the others throw them bread, he was no zookeeper.

I gave her a roll from the bag I had and she held it out for a baboon to snatch. (He didn't take, he grabbed.) "You might at least say 'Thank you,'" Roxanne called after him.

Down the path a ways, there was a loud screech and we turned as a big grandfather baboon with graying hair went shrieking and scampering down to the pond where, still mewling, he washed out his mouth with water.

There was laughter, but it was momentary. An angry Mr. Gelston, astride the middle of the path, was commanding our attention again. "Back to the bus," he ordered. "We're going back to the bus. I *told* you you're to treat the animals kindly. Someone fed that baboon a roll filled with hot pepper. I *told* you that's not what Africa and this safari trip are about. People like that should stay home and run over cats."

We were shooed back to the bus, all of us sobered with the exception of Richard. "What do you mean with all this highhandedness?" he demanded of Gelston when we boarded. "I hadn't even begun to see what's in the damned park!"

"Sorry," Gelston answered coldly, "but that kind of treatment of animals cannot be countenanced. These creatures, and Kenya's offering them to tourists, are something to be appreciated. Kenya does not want them harmed or made fun of, and certainly not tortured."

"That stupid baboon wasn't *tortured*," Richard railed. "Just because someone wanted to have a little fun, you don't have to start acting like a high priest."

"Kenya's attitude is that these animals are to be protected and viewed for pleasure, not for torture and killing. That's why game hunting is not allowed here."

"Stop it," Richard ordered. "Who do you think you're lecturing to? Do you think I came all the way over from America to listen to you talk? I came here to see *animals* and you want to tell me they should be better treated than humans." Richard pointed his finger. (At Cartwright Company, it was supposed to make an employee tremble.) "I'm reminding you, Mr. Gelston, that it's *tourism* that keeps this country afloat, and it's *American tourism* that keeps the Holcomb Travel Agency afloat! And I'm telling *you*—" the

knifelike finger was aimed, "that if travel agents and
bleeding heart animal-lovers are going to treat tourists like
schoolchildren, Kenya's going to find itself without a tourist trade."

Richard sat down beside his wife with a satisfied smile.
Samantha chose to view the passing scenery.

BACK AT THE HOTEL, well in time for lunch, the group de-
barked. Gelston was glum, Richard haughty, Samantha
keeping to herself. Roxanne, Dagger, and I were the last to
leave the bus and she leaned over the driver. "I'm sorry
we've made you unhappy," she told him. "You were smiling before. You aren't smiling now. I prefer it when you
smile."

Amram Kitanyi did not look up. He stared at the curve of
the drive ahead, his face somber. "I shall smile again," he
told her. "For whatever good it might do."

"Good?" she asked. "What do you mean?"

He shook his head slowly. "I have a feeling," he said,
"that what has happened with this group thus far is *not* a
good omen for the success of this tour."

I DON'T KNOW what the others did, but I sacked out until
time for Lise Smith's slide show on birds at 6:00. I hoped I'd
see Roxanne and the colonel there, but outside of the bird
watchers and myself, the only others present were Marshall
and Sylvia Benedict and Neville Street and, at that, Neville
left halfway through. I think he, too, was hoping Roxanne
would attend.

The slides were pretty, but the show was the kind that
would only interest bird lovers. There were pictures of the
black-collared barbet, the red-fronted parrot, the pale-
chanting goshawk, and more other strange-feathered friends
than I cared to note down. Lise Smith, whose husband ran

the slide projector, knew more about those birds than I know about my relatives. But then, she'd been in Kenya twenty-five years.

I ate dinner with the Benedicts and I didn't see Roxanne and the colonel until I went back to my room. Then, to my surprise, I found them both there, having a drink and laughing about something. He was holding a glass and leaning on his gold-headed cane. Roxanne was in the chair by the windows and was wearing a long flowing white cotton print she jokingly remarked would be the last bit of feminine garb she'd be donning for the next ten days. It was low-cut, sleeveless, and billowy, and as she lounged, legs crossed, rhinestone earrings catching the light, the multi-bracelets on her wrists, I couldn't take my eyes off her.

"Just in time for a drink with us," the colonel greeted me. "How was the slide show?"

I said I'd like a drink, and the slide show was for the birds. "But how did you know I went to the slide show?"

The colonel, putting his cane on the bed and going to the bureau to pour an inch of Scotch into a glass, followed by two inches of soda and ice cubes from a bucket on the dresser, said, "You're writing a travel article about this safari trip. You're thorough in your work. I take it for granted you'll attend any program that's offered."

"That's another thing I don't understand," I said, accepting the drink. "How did you find out I'm writing a travel article? That was supposed to be a secret."

He picked up and wielded his cane, stroked the handle, and rested the tip on the floor. "If that be the case," he said, "fear not. I won't betray you."

"But how did you find out?"

That gave the colonel momentary pause. "I don't know," he answered slowly. "I hadn't thought about it." He rested one hand on the cane, rubbed his chin, and looked at his daughter, who was awaiting his answer as expectantly as I.

"Come tell us," Roxanne said, beaming. "I want to hear, too."

"Let me see," the colonel answered, now leaning both hands on his cane. "I enter the airport waiting room. A man is sitting against the wall, notebook in hand. He's not a bird watcher, for the ones who are, are talking to Busby Morgan, the tour director, and to each other about the trip. I meet the group. Busby tells me the man sitting by himself is named James Addison, who's filling the one vacancy left on the tour. Sidney Leggett tells me James Addison doesn't know what a life-list is.

"It doesn't take much brains to figure that the vacancy was reserved by some large organization which wasn't sure whom they'd assign to fill it, but 'bird watching' wasn't one of the criteria. 'James Addison' is a byline I've seen on articles a number of times. Poultry raising, as I recall. I confess I didn't read that one. The traffic problem in New York? That one I did."

Colonel Dagger played with his cane a little, studying the glance of light off its golden head, and I watched the admiring way his daughter's eyes followed him. "So," he said, picking up his drink, turning to toast me with cane and glass, "when James Addison's name is on the list of an African safari group, what am I to believe about a man who writes on such diverse subjects as chickens and traffic and— I believe you did one on stained glass—but that he's on assignment to do an article about African safaris?"

I admitted he was right and had to concede the deduction wasn't all that difficult once he'd explained it. I felt as opaque as a pane of glass.

Roxanne said, "Tell him what else you've done, Papa."

He laughed. "Oh, that." To me he said, "I took the liberty, without consulting you, of asking that we three ride together in the same van over the next ten days. If you have strong objections, it can be changed, of course."

"I can't think of anything I'd like better," I answered, toasting them in return.

Roxanne was not content. "Won't you tell him the rest, Papa? Tell him why."

The colonel shook his head. "It's your game, Daughter. *You* tell him."

She was embarrassed. A becoming pink flitted across her face. "My father," she said hesitantly, "fears for my safety. He thinks I've come into a den of wolves."

"To put it succinctly," the colonel told me, "those hungry bachelors, Peter Tower and Neville Street, out of that terrible Cartwright Company, want to play games with my daughter." He gave Roxanne the grimace of a smile, but her return smile was as warm as an oven. "If she wants to play games," the colonel went on, "she can do it on her *own* time, when she's out of my ken. I'm an old-fashioned father, as I told you."

Roxanne smiled fondly at him and lifted her glass. "I'm a little old-fashioned too, Papa," she confided. "Besides, I'm forewarned and forearmed. I read Jim's article on New York as a bachelor's paradise!" She gave me the wickedest, most knowing smile of all.

ROXANNE LEFT as soon as she'd finished her drink and the colonel got ready for bed. First he laid the gold-headed cane gently across his coverlet, as if it might get scratched, then started shedding his clothes.

On my own bed I took off my shoes. "That cane," I said, "is the most beautiful object I've ever seen."

"Perhaps not quite the equal of Tutankhamen's gold mask," he smiled, sitting to remove his own shoes. Unshoeing his left foot caused a slight difficulty he pretended was clumsiness. "But I do treasure it," he continued. "I'd be lost without it."

"Might I look at it?"

He nodded, but only after a moment of hesitation. "Of course." He handed it to me, head end first, and went into the bathroom to shower.

It was *heavy*! It wasn't just the gold head. The black wood that made up its mass was dense and twice the diameter of normal canes. To carry it was to be constantly aware of its presence. Just by hefting it I could see why the colonel made it part of his equipage. Once you're used to having it, you can't get used to *not* having it.

I wondered if a sword were sheathed inside its massive girth and turned the cane around and around looking for a secret button. I didn't see such a thing, but I did discover a small inscription on the underside of the handle which read: "To Jesse Dakar—*Adventure in Terror*—Cast & Crew."

I HAD TO READ the words three times before it dawned on me what they meant. I put the cane carefully back on the bed and poured myself another drink—a double!

The colonel came out in the pair of boxer shorts that formed his sleeping attire and I said, "I read the inscription on the handle of your cane."

"Oh, yes?" he said, and poured himself another drink, also a double.

"You *are* Jesse Dakar?"

He took his glass to the bed and picked up the cane. "That name mean anything to you?"

"*Mean* anything to me?" I told him then about reading the manuscript of his last book over ten years ago, how it

had made me want to write, turned me into a newspaperman with the urge to author books. And I told him what
little I knew about "Jesse Dakar," that he'd been a private
detective, served in Vietnam, retiring with the rank of colonel, writing four mystery novels, having a Hollywood career converting his mysteries into movies, following which
he went on to further fame and fortune as a screenwriter.
"Jesse Dakar" had been one of the most famous names in
Hollywood.

He listened thoughtfully, sitting on the edge of the bed,
leaning on his cane, staring at the floor. When he looked up,
he said, "Now we both know secrets about each other. May
I request that you not reveal my florid past to the rest of the
group? I much prefer traveling under my real name, Japheth
Dagger, and especially under the sobriquet 'Colonel.' I'm
afraid that, if my 'Jesse Dakar' pseudonym were known, I'd
find myself attracting a lot of attention I want to avoid."

"Of course," I answered. "You're Colonel Japheth
Dagger, The Philosophers Club, New York City."

"Just 'Colonel,'" he said. "I keep my given name as secret as my pseudonym. I hate it. And I shall call you
James."

I had a hundred questions to ask him. Why hadn't he
written a book in a dozen years? Why no screenplays? What
about Vietnam? His wounds? (That hideous scar on his left
leg!) His recent divorce? The other things his daughter had
mentioned?

And what about his long career as a top detective in
Brandt's, one of the world's largest private investigation
agencies? (No wonder he figured me out so readily.)

But he was not a man who talked about himself. Right
then he was bidding me good night and turning in.

SEVEN

Sunday, June 22

FOUR WHITE DATSUN VANS with raisable roofs and Kenyan drivers, Amram Kitanyi among them, were lined up in the hotel drive at quarter of eight the following morning when the tour group came out from breakfast with all its equipment, ready to travel. Colonel Dagger had invited me to share a van with him and Roxanne, but he hadn't made any further selections and I discovered, to my horror, when Amram, who was our driver, started to load the baggage, that the other couple who would ride with us were Richard and Samantha Cartwright. That put a fast damper on the pleasure I anticipated at riding with the beauteous Roxanne, and at the green, gnawing jealousy Neville Street and Peter Tower would share.

Richard and Samantha hadn't occurred to me. I assumed they'd be riding with the old man. Foolish thinking.

So I stood on the sidewalk beside our van, watching Amram stow Cartwright luggage along with Dagger and Addison bags into the rear compartment behind the back passenger seat. Already my trip was spoiled.

The vans pulled out in a line at 8:00 sharp for the Masai Mara Game Preserve, and Amram led the way on the first leg of the journey, which paused at 8:45 on the A104 for a view of the Rift Valley and the crater of the distant Susua volcano. Richard rode by himself in the rear, Samantha took the middle seat, Dagger and I the first seats by the panel door, and Roxanne elected to ride up front beside Amram, where she could see best and fire him endless questions. Like her father, she was after information, but, instead of deducing it, she asked for it, begged for it, queried for it. And she had picked the right spot. Amram was voluble, knowledgeable, and quick-eyed. At 110 km/hr, he could point out a Hildebrandt's starling on a tree stump, or a lilac-breasted roller on a twig, and stop to give us a chance for a photograph. It was wasted on all but Roxanne. She kept wanting more, and what Amram knew about birds, animals, and Kenya was more than I could put in a book. Roxanne was enthralled.

The colonel and I, a seat behind, couldn't hear all they talked about, but her eyes darted everywhere, and Amram was guiding and monitoring her in his soft-spoken voice, only occasionally pointing out something to the rest of us.

Watching the performance, all I could think was that Roxanne exuded a charm that laid all men at her feet. Not just young white Americans like Peter Tower, Neville Street, and me. Though he would have denied it, I even think she owned her father!

NATIVE HAWKERS swarmed around us at the Rift Valley Punta Vista, offering soapstone candle holders, flower vases, animal carvings. Most passengers were intrigued, except for Richard Cartwright, who railed at them, berating the lot to begone, ordering them to disperse and retire to their homes as if he, Richard Cartwright, had taken over the country!

I watched Samantha during this. She didn't get out of the van.

ON OUR WAY AGAIN, we dipped down and crossed the Rift Valley, halting at 10:15 for a half-hour pit and rest stop at the town of Narok and we reached the gates of the Masai

Mara game park at noon. Now we saw wild animals: baboons, impalas crossing the road, ostriches, warthogs, and at a water hole we witnessed a mother hyena attacking one of her young, despite the van drivers stopping and throwing rocks trying to drive her off. The cub went whimpering away, a leg broken, and Amram said it wouldn't live long.

"Why would she attack her own baby?" Roxanne wondered.

"When food is scarce," Amram answered, "they'll devour their cubs."

THE FOUR VANS reached the Masai Mara Lodge at quarter of two. It crested a steep slope that looked down on distant plains where, barely visible without binoculars, a half-dozen giraffe strolled. The tourist quarters, stuccoed units with single windows overlooking the slope and back doors to a rear path, spread down the hillside a hundred yards on both sides of the lodge, odds to the left, evens to the right, and when we checked in, there was an immediate outcry from Phineas. He'd been given the key to cabin no. 5 and as soon as he left the veranda in the wake of the porter, he discovered it was third down the slope, and back he came. He was damned, he said, if was going to walk down and up any slopes when cabin no. 1 was at the crest. He wanted cabin no. 1.

The Kenyan registration clerk explained in clear, precise English that it was quite impossible. Cabins no. 1 and no. 3 were already occupied by earlier arrivals. Cabin no. 5 was the nearest to the lodge of those remaining.

"Don't you tell me what's where, you black scum," Phineas retaliated. "Stick whoever you've put in cabin one down in cabin five. I'm seventy-five years old and I'm not walking up and down any hills."

"Sir," the clerk replied, struggling to maintain his politeness, "I don't have the power to change rooms. I can only assign them. And yours is the one that's closest to the lodge. It's only about thirty meters."

"Meters? Don't feed me that foreign stuff. It's down a hill and I'm not walking on hills. I *told* you I want cabin one. I don't care what you do or how you do it, but get it for me. You understand?"

The clerk was beginning to buckle. "Sir," he said, a plaintive plea in his voice. "I can't do anything like that. I have no power."

Phineas turned to Busby. "You're the one in charge here. You're supposed to be running this safari. *You* get me cabin number one!" He pointed a finger that was far more formidable than his son's. "Make no mistake," he said. "When I booked this tour, I laid down conditions. You know what they are. And you know equally well, that if they're not rigorously met, you and your whole goddam program are going to be sued. I have an ironclad contract, and if you don't think it's ironclad, talk to George Gamble. He's right here to tell you. And it says in black and white that if you go against my wishes in any way, you are liable." He pointed his finger again. "And when I say you're liable, I mean I'm going to leave your operation bankrupt."

That had Busby hurrying off to see the manager while the rest of us shifted our feet in the lobby surrounded by our baggage and waiting porters.

After fifteen minutes, Busby came back. He had, he said, with a choking swallow, been able to arrange for cabin no. 1 to be made available for Phineas Cartwright.

That brought only a momentary sigh of relief, for now it was Richard's turn. If his father could acquire the cabin at the head of the slope, the one closest to the lodge, then

Richard Cartwright was determined to have the next one in
line. Never mind that that, also, had been previously assigned. Another change had to be structured. If Phineas got
cabin no. 1, he was to have cabin no. 3.

So we in the group cooled our heels another ten minutes
while more negotiations went on. At the end, it was announced that Phineas Cartwright would inhabit cabin no.
1, sharing it with Duncan Hawley, while Richard and Samantha Cartwright would disport themselves in cabin no. 3.
As for the rest of us, Colonel Dagger and I were assigned to
cabin 13, seventh down the hill, and Roxanne and Lise
Smith were adjacent in cabin 15.

The manager, a tall, lean, unctuous Kenyan named David Mozamba, whose smile was as genuine as a twenty-
dollar diamond ring, came out of his office with Busby to
assure Richard that the change had been made, and Mr. and
Mrs. Cartwright would spend their night in cabin 3. To the
rest of us he apologized with a grandiose show of concern
for the delay.

We guests flowed down to our cabins at last, then returned to the lodge for lunch. By now, the lunch hour was
long past, but lunch was part of the itinerary and the help
had to stay on and provide. It was a meal eaten in silence.

THERE WAS an afternoon game drive over the fields at four,
and Roxanne rode up front with Amram again.

My boss, Bill Clayborn, was wrong when he said we
wouldn't come within a thousand yards of a lion. We drove
up and parked so close to a pride of two males and four females sleeping under a tree I was afraid we'd run over their
cubs. In minutes, eight other vans were ringing the dozing
adults, but all they did was open an eye and go back to sleep.

"They look so cute I'd like to reach out and pet them,"
Roxanne said.

"If you did, we'd call you 'lefty,'" Amram grinned.

"But they don't pay any attention to us."

"They don't know what's inside the van is edible. They think we're just movable scenery."

"It doesn't seem to frighten them."

"A lion doesn't know how to be afraid. He's got nothing to be afraid of. Except us. But he doesn't know that."

"If I had a gun," Richard snorted, "I'd make him afraid! I'd turn his damned yellow eyes red with terror."

"If you had a gun," Amram muttered quietly, "I'd suggest you shoot him from *inside* the van."

WE SAW A LEOPARD, too, up in a tree by himself. I counted thirty-four vans and one Mercedes Benz crowded around. Maybe we won't shoot those great carnivores. Maybe we'll just hound them to death.

We saw a lot of other animals, too. Thompson gazelles, zebra, grazing topis—they always have one of their number standing on a little mound, facing in the direction of the lions, doing sentry duty.

But who cares about the other animals when you can see lions, or a leopard. Those great cats did no more than yawn, but they were the ones we hung around.

"They sleep twenty-two hours a day," Amram explained on the way back. "Because they have a high protein diet, they only need to eat every couple of days. Grass is low in protein. Grazing animals have to eat all day long."

EIGHT

Sunday, June 22

WHEN AMRAM RETURNED US to the lodge, it was half past six and getting dark. Kenya's on the equator and, all year round, winter and summer, the days and nights are twelve hours long. I had time for a shower before joining Roxanne and the colonel for a drink at seven-fifteen. Dinner was at eight and we got a table by ourselves, then went onto the terrace for coffee.

A full moon was rising above the ridge, blindingly bright. The sky was a baby blue, there was the breath of a breeze, the stillness of a desert, the soft fragrance of flowers. It was a night for love.

Roxanne was between me and the colonel, crowded around a tiny table by the railing overlooking the slope, the tourist quarters, and the distant plains. Roxanne had laughed that she wouldn't be wearing female attire for the rest of the tour but here she was in that low-cut, sleeveless, billowy white print of last night, the earrings, the jangle of bracelets, and a hint of perfume that made her almost impossible not to embrace.

Our knees touched under the table. Nothing deliberate. I wondered if she might let them stay together, but she didn't. She wasn't a girl you could move in on. There was a reserve about her that said, "Don't get serious. Keep everything light." We three sipped coffee, inhaled the magic of the evening, and said little.

Soft music started and couples rose to dance on the broad sweep of terrace behind us. The colonel, who, resting one arm on the railing, had the best view, toyed idly with his cane and observed, "Here comes trouble."

Roxanne laughed and didn't turn around. "Which one?" she asked, "Mr. Street, or Mr. Tower?" To me, she confided, "I'm not being a detective. That comes from knowing Papa."

"Both, but they're temporarily intimidated. They don't like the scowl on my face."

"Papa wants me to be an old maid," Roxanne told me.

The colonel replied, "Any reasonably intelligent girl with your looks would have been married a decade since and I wouldn't have to worry." He went on to me. "When I was seventeen, my father told me that every girl from the age of fourteen on views every boy she goes out with as a potential husband. I didn't believe him because I was heavily into girls—for anything *but* marriage. But I came to find out he was right. There's only one exception to that rule. My daughter."

"Well, then," she answered, patting his hand, "why do you worry?"

"I worry," he said, "because you're *not* married."

The piece ended, and as couples paused on the dance floor, awaiting the next number, up stood Phineas Cartwright. He was with Richard and Samantha and he was either drunk or angry. "What the hell are we doing here?" he yelled. "I thought this was supposed to be *Africa*! What the hell are you people playing American music for? We get enough of that junk at home! Why don't you play *African* music? That's what we came here for! Why don't you bring out your damned tom-toms and have the natives do the dancing?"

Waiters and management hurried around him, but he shook them off. "I'm sick of this American stuff. I thought I was going to see *Africa.*" When they tried to quiet him, he yelled, "Get your hands off me. I'm going to sue. I'll sue the lot of you." With that, he stormed off the terrace toward his cabin no. 1 at the head of the slope, yelling, "I'll sue you, you damned black bastards," as they followed in his wake.

After calm had been restored, the music began again. I turned to ask Roxanne to dance when, from out of nowhere, Neville Street was between us, presenting her with the same request.

Roxanne didn't notice my offer. Away she went on Neville's arm, and in a moment they were dancing together, infuriatingly close, while I was left sitting with the colonel like an extra chaperon.

Why I had two left feet around that girl doesn't speak well of someone who wrote a well-praised, in-depth article on the pros and cons of New York as a bachelor's paradise, most of it from personal experience! But she had an uncomfortable way of making me feel more Dagger's generation than her own.

The colonel and I ordered Scotch and sodas.

The terrace grew crowded with dancers, many from other tour groups, but some from our own. I spotted the bird-watching couples, the Kirbys and Baldwins, at a table together, swapping partners. Sidney Leggett wasn't around. He'd gone to bed, for Busby Morgan and Lise Smith were leading a bird-watching tour of the area at six-thirty tomorrow morning.

Richard and Samantha Cartwright were dancing, if you could call the arm's length at which they held each other "dancing." Occasionally I caught glimpses of Roxanne, first in Neville's arms, then Peter's, over on the other side, as far from Dagger as they could manage. Ultimately, I got up and circulated. I was as bad as the colonel. I wanted to check up on her, see what she was doing.

No one was at the Neville-Peter table when I cruised the area, but it held a bucket of ice, three glasses, soda, and a 1.75 liter of whiskey. I guessed they were trying to get her drunk.

I didn't report that to the colonel when I returned, however. I only sat down uneasily. The colonel ordered us another round of drinks and brooded.

Duncan Hawley danced by with Lucy Children, and she was half a head taller. Next he danced with Jennifer Long, and they were the same height. The two women, Lucy and Jennifer, were alone at a table adjacent to the dance floor, but the only one to approach them was Duncan. He spent the rest of the time inside the bar.

The Gambles and Benedicts shared a table, and both danced, but huge Marshall only danced with tiny Sylvie, and George danced only with dark-eyed Harriet.

And *there* was Roxanne, in the arms of Peter Tower again! Enough was enough. I got up and cut in.

Peter gave me a dirty look when Roxanne let him go, but she smiled as she came into my arms. "So you dance?"

"Only with someone like you."

That made her laugh.

We fitted closely, like gloves, her steps mingling with mine so that we floated without effort. I held her close and she said, "A moment. Let me have just one deep breath." Then she let me pull her close again and I could sense the appeal of her perfume, the brush of her earlobe against my lips, the feel of her softness pressing hard against me. I hadn't been this affected by a girl since high school.

"Over here," she whispered, and directed me near a corner. George and Harriet Gamble were quarreling by a post, and Roxanne wanted to eavesdrop.

"That's enough," Harriet was saying. "You've done absolutely enough."

"Nowhere near enough," he answered harshly. "I haven't begun to fight. You'll see."

"I'll see *nothing*," she retorted, beauteous in her gown. Next to Roxanne, Harriet Gamble was the most attractive woman in the lodge. And now she turned from her husband, headed for the end of the terrace, and started down the walk to the cabins.

He made no attempt to follow her. Instead, he went the other way, into the bar.

"Is that the fairy-tale story of marriage?" Roxanne laughed as she swung away again in my arms.

"What's that?"

"In fairy tales, marriage is the end. Everyone lives happily ever after. Isn't it, instead, only the beginning? The horrors come *after* the wedding, not before?"

"What can you know? You've never been married."

"But my father was married three times. And each was worse than the one before."

"Some marriages are happy."

She laughed and put her lips to my ear. "And how many times have *you* been married, pray tell?"

"I'm an idealist."

"Too bad," she answered, and pulled me in another direction. "Here's more grist for the mill." She indicated Richard and Samantha Cartwright, who were separating close by.

"I've had it," Richard told Samantha. "Father was right. Dancing is for the Africans. It's time we called it a night."

"Time for *you* to call it a night, sweet," she cooed with hatred in her eye. "It's only quarter past ten. Do you *really* think I'm going to exchange this place for a room with you at this hour?"

"I don't give a damn *what* you do." He flung his arms. "Stay up all night for all I care. I'm turning in right now."

"Sleep well," she taunted. "I won't wake you when I come to bed. It'd be impossible."

Richard turned away, fury on his face, and she laughed in scorn as he went.

I wanted to digest this delicious piece with Roxanne, but Neville's heavy hand landed on my shoulder. *He* wanted to dance with the maiden fair. I would have dueled with him, but she had already bid me a smiling "thank you" and was off and away in his arms once more, back to him and Peter—and that huge bottle of whiskey.

I returned to the colonel.

"The wolves are relentless," he said as I sat down.

"My guess is she's no lamb."

"I wish I shared your confidence."

"How old is she?" I queried.

"Twenty-eight. A vulnerable age."

"Colonel, I have to tell you. You were born in a different time."

"And, James, I have to tell *you*, time has nothing to do with it."

"Your daughter's perfectly able to take care of herself."

"As *I'm* able to take care of *myself*. She doesn't believe it of me, and I don't believe it of her."

A waiter, carrying a bottle and glass on a tray, darted off the terrace, down to the cabins. I watched until he disappeared and said, "Guess who that's for?"

The colonel was more interested in what Neville Street and Peter Tower were doing. Right then, while Neville held Roxanne tightly in his arms, Peter was doing the same with Samantha Cartwright, holding her just as close.

I commented, "Here's where Peter beats out Neville. Neville wants Roxanne, but Peter wants next year's salesmanship award. That's the way to get it. It's called play up to the boss's wife.''

"Or," said the colonel, "if the cat's away, the mice will play."

I CUT IN on Roxanne and Neville about the time the black waiter returned from the cabins banging his empty tray against his knee. Neville didn't return to his table as I expected, but took Samantha away from Peter. I was sure Peter would then head my way but the band took a break and I escaped with Roxanne back to the colonel.

"See," she said to her father, spreading her arms with a cheery smile as she took her seat. "Still in one piece."

Across the way, George Gamble emerged from the bar and stalked off the terrace toward his quarters with a glower that boded ill for Harriet. Twenty minutes of drinking had fortified whatever resolve he needed.

The Benedicts paused by our table when the music resumed to tell us they were turning in. "It's quarter of eleven," Marshall explained, "and we want to get up for that bird walk tomorrow morning."

They went down the path, and Duncan Hawley emerging from the bar, weaving a little, followed after.

Half the tables were empty now. It was close to eleven after a long, wearying day and the evening was winding down. Even Neville and Peter seemed willing to adjourn their battle for Roxanne's affections.

THEN DUNCAN HAWLEY, the short, frowzled, head-of-production of the Cartwright Company, who'd just weaved off to the quarters he shared with Phineas Cartwright, came hurrying back up the path, totally sobered.

"Where's Busby Morgan?" he cried out. "Is anyone here a doctor?"

Colonel Dagger rose to his feet. "What's the trouble?"

"Phineas Cartwright's ill. Quick! I think he's had a heart attack."

NINE

DAGGER WAS off the terrace in an instant, past the distraught Hawley and down the path, Roxanne and I at his heels. Hawley's face had an ashen cast and, back among the dancers, there was stunned silence.

The louvred door of cabin no. 1 was wide open when Roxanne and I arrived, and Dagger was on his knees checking the pulse of a prone Phineas Cartwright, who lay on his back between the dresser and the beds. As we got to him, the colonel ripped open the man's shirt, thrusting away an impeding tie to bare Phineas's chest, and put an ear to his heart.

"An ambulance?" I said, ready to run for help.

Dagger raised up, a strange expression on his face. He bent and sniffed at the man's lips, then rose to his knees, a dark scowl on his brow. His glance swept the room.

"No," he answered. "The man's dead. He's been poisoned."

Dagger picked up a drinking glass from the floor beside the body, smelled it, and came to his feet.

Duncan Hawley peered hesitantly through the door. Behind him was a clamor of voices.

"Don't come in," Dagger ordered Phineas's roommate. "Keep everybody out!"

I pushed Duncan back. "Block the door. Nobody's to come in."

Roxanne was by the bed now, ignoring the dead man, watching her father.

Dagger had picked up a liqueur bottle from the bureau, the one I'd seen the porter bearing down the path not more than half an hour before, and was sniffing its mouth. He turned the bottle this way and that, studying its label. "'Père Javineau,'" he read. "That's an uncommon brand." He bent to look at the bottom. Then he reset it on the bureau beside its cork, a card, and Phineas's room key.

"Did you say *poisoned*?" Duncan whispered from the doorway, and the word was echoed among the curious behind him.

"It's poison," Dagger announced and went to the man, leaning confidentially close. "Get the manager down here. Tell him Mr. Cartwright's dead, that it's cyanide poison and he should telephone the police. Then wake up Richard Cartwright and Busby Morgan. Tell them what's happened."

Duncan, bearing a message to Garcia, hurried out and up the path, murmuring, "Phineas. Cyanide" to those he passed.

I ignored the cries of the curious, locked the door, and turned. Dagger had picked up the large card that had accompanied the bottle. He turned it one way and the other. "Compliments of the Holcomb Travel Agency," he read from it dryly and put it back in place.

On the floor between us, Phineas Cartwright lay stretched, legs and arms extended, his jacket open, shirt ripped wide, his tie askew. Thick gray hair matted his bared chest, his eyes stared sightlessly at the ceiling, his mouth gaped. He was ugly when alive, he was uglier dead.

Roxanne, however, was not repelled. "Cyanide poison?" she said to her father. "In that bottle?"

He nodded. "Cyanide. It's full of it." He leaned both hands heavily on the cane in what I came to know was a sign of thought. "How the hell," he said, "would cyanide get into a liqueur bottle in the middle of Africa?"

"Who'd want to murder him?" Roxanne asked.

The colonel gave her a sudden, amused smile. "I think it'd be easier to answer, 'Who wouldn't?'" He picked up and read the card again. "'Compliments of the Holcomb Travel Agency,'" he snorted. "What kind of a blind is that? Amateur night!" He relaid his cane on the counterpane, knelt, and went through the dead man's pockets.

Roxanne said, "Is this Masai Mara Lodge's way of paying him back for all the trouble he caused?"

There were voices and questions outside and someone said, "I'm a doctor. Is there anything I can do?"

"No!" I called. "Thanks all the same."

The doctor's voice was against the other side of the door. "Let me see the patient."

"The man is dead. You can't come in."

"Who says he's dead? I insist on seeing for myself. I'm a doctor."

"Colonel Dagger says he's dead. What's your name, Doctor? Where're you from? What hospital are you with?"

There was no answer, just a movement away from the door. Amazing how people back off when asked to identify themselves!

I had time now, so I tried to play detective à la Colonel Dagger and see what clues I might spot. I pulled aside the curtain hiding the small closet. The hangers were empty and heavy suitcases where on the floor. Three had Phineas's name on them, one was Duncan Hawley's.

Dagger, searching the body, produced a piece of paper from the right-hand jacket pocket, which he unfolded and read aloud. "'I must talk to you. As soon as possible. It's vital.'" He turned that over, front and back, and announced, "No signature." He handed it to Roxanne. "Woman's writing, wouldn't you say?"

She studied it. "It's got a smallness, a smoothness to it. It's probably a woman. But who?" she handed it back.

"Someone in the Cartwright group. Given to him today. The paper's fresh; hasn't been in his pocket long. Not lodge or hotel stationery, though. From a notebook."

"Lucy Children was his personal secretary," I said.

"Not too likely she'd be sending him notes then." Dagger replaced the paper in the pocket he'd found it in.

I went over the other Cartwright women in my mind: Jennifer Long, bookkeeper. Then there were the wives: Samantha Cartwright, Sylvia Benedict, and Harriet Gamble. Could it have been one of them? Perhaps Samantha.

Dagger searched quickly through the dead man's other pockets, assessing and replacing. He didn't sort through Phineas's wallet or examine anything, just checked what he carried.

David Mozamba, the tall, oily manager of the Masai Mara Lodge, waked untimely from his bed, knocked, and identified himself.

I unbarred the door and he greeted us with the same shifty-eyed unctuousness he'd displayed when apologizing to the tour group about the registration dispute. He wore the same business suit, the same phony smile, the same appeasing manner.

"Yes?" he said, looking first at us, and then at the body. "Mr. Cartwright is dead?" From the way he said it, Phineas Cartwright might have been an ant Mr. Mozamba had inadvertently stepped upon.

"Dead," the colonel answered. "He's been poisoned. Cyanide." He pointed. "It's in that bottle there. Have you notified the police? I asked Mr. Hawley to advise you."

Mr. Mozamba's manner developed a glint of hauteur. He didn't have to bow and scrape to *everybody*. "Pray tell," he said, and his grin was stronger. "I do not call authorities without personal observation. The nearest police are in Narok, more than a two-hour drive away. I must know for myself before I involve Captain Lumumba. Captain Lumumba is not a man to be disturbed for little reason." He dared to turn his smile upon the colonel.

The colonel, leaning one hand on his cane, gestured at the body. "Then do please observe, Mr. Mozamba. Mr. Cartwright is an important man back in the United States and he's very dead." Dagger snatched the liqueur bottle from the dresser and held out its mouth for Mozamba to sniff. "This is what killed him, Mr. Mozamba. He drank of this, here in this room, out of that glass, in this lodge, delivered to him by one of your waiters. I think Captain Lumumba would want to hear about this right away."

Mr. Mozamba's smile was replaced by rapid blinking. "One of my waiters?" He gestured at the body. "One of my waiters did this?"

"We do not know *who* did it," the colonel answered. "But it has been done."

"Which of my waiters?"

"I think that's for Captain Lumumba to decide."

Mr. Mozamba nodded and gave us his twenty-dollar diamond ring smile. There could be a new manager at the Masai Mara Lodge if he made one false move.

"Yes," he agreed. "I shall have to call Captain Lumumba." He turned, shoulders slumped, to the door and turned again. "Colonel, sir. The captain may want to question you over the phone. Perhaps you will come to the lodge with me?"

Colonel Dagger nodded and hefted his cane, studying for a moment its golden head. "If you wish."

TEN

THE NUMBER of the curious had diminished when Roxanne, the colonel, and I left the dead man's quarters. The time was quarter past eleven. Peter Tower, Neville Street, Samantha Cartwright, George Gamble, and Marshall Benedict were there, over by the edge of the path in quiet conversation. But their number was now augmented by the appearance of a half-dressed Richard Cartwright storming out of the adjacent quarters in response to the message he'd received from Duncan Hawley.

"What's this about my father?" Richard shouted, coming around to where the colonel was turning the key in Phineas's lock. "Here! What do you think you're doing? Unlock that door!"

The colonel pocketed the key. "I'm sorry. No one's to go in there until Captain Lumumba arrives."

"You aren't giving me orders! That's my father in there!"

Dagger was quiet about it. "I know, and your father's been murdered. No one's to touch anything inside that room until the police come."

Richard could barely restrain himself from seizing the tall, older man. "And who the hell do you think you're giving orders to?"

"To you. I can understand your grief, but try to control yourself." Dagger turned to Samantha, "Perhaps you have some sedatives he can take. Try to comfort him."

Richard was so apoplectic he was speechless, and in that moment while his mouth hung open, the colonel started up the path. Richard, having lost him, swung back to his own quarters, regaining his voice just in time to turn and point a finger at Dagger's receding back and shout, "You're going to hear about this!" He stormed inside and slammed the door.

Samantha, her mouth tight, said reluctantly to nobody in particular, "I'd better go tend to him." It was a task she didn't relish and she moved sluggishly in his direction as Roxanne and I started after the colonel.

UP AT THE REGISTRATION DESK, David Mozamba was making his phone call, conversing in Swahili and mopping his brow with a snow-white handkerchief. He put down the phone, a grayish cast to his black face. "Captain Lumumba had nothing to ask you," he told Dagger. "The captain has ordered that the room be locked, that all guests be available for questioning when he arrives." Mozamba looked at his watch. "He should be here in two to three hours. And he's very angry."

Colonel Dagger wasn't interested in the state of Captain Lumumba's temper. "Who ordered the bottle to be delivered to Mr. Cartwright?" he demanded.

"I don't know," the manager whined. "Maybe Mr. Cartwright ordered it himself."

"Where's the waiter who delivered it?"

"I don't know which waiter it was. They're all in bed now. You'll have to excuse me." Mozamba tried to regain control by making notes. "Captain Lumumba wants arrangements made to take care of the body. I'll have to notify Mr. Richard Cartwright. And Mr. Morgan, the tour director. Let me see, Mr. Hawley will have to be given another room."

Richard, now dressed, burst in at that moment and stormed over to the manager. "What the hell kind of a hotel are you running here? What do you mean, letting guests get poisoned? Is this Kenya's way of treating tourists?"

Mr. Mozamba had a defense at last. "Captain Lumumba's in charge now," he explained. "Captain Lumumba is the one to make your complaints to. He's head of police in this area. He'll be here in a couple of hours."

"I'm not just going to complain about you and your manner, I'm going to make a complaint against that so-called colonel who locks me out of my father's room."

I turned for Dagger's response, but the colonel wasn't there. Roxanne looked, too, and we looked at each other. It was as if he'd disappeared.

Now a worried Busby Morgan crossed the outer terrace and joined us. "This is terrible," he said. "Nobody's ever died on one of my tours before."

I kept looking for Dagger. Finally I found him, in the now-closed bar, talking to the bartender who was cleaning up. He came out again.

"You're the one," Richard said, advancing on Dagger with outstretched finger, the one that was supposed to evoke terror.

Dagger cut him off. "Sorry about your father," he said, and turned to the tour leader. "Sorry about all this, Busby." Then he said to Richard, "Did you hear your father die?"

Richard, his finger wavering uselessly, said, "What?"

"When you left the party and said you were going to retire, did you go directly to your room?"

Richard stared for a moment. Then he erupted. "Of course I did. When I say I'm going to retire, where the *hell* do you *think* I'm going to go?"

"So you were in your quarters when the bottle of liqueur was delivered to your father next door?"

"How do *I* know when the bottle was delivered?" He leaned toward Dagger, glowering his fiercest threat. "What are you driving at, Dagger?"

"I want to find out if you heard anything—if he cried out."

"Through those thick walls? How the hell could you expect me to hear anything? I didn't know anything was going on until Duncan Hawley told me." Richard made an effort to regain command and the swordlike finger came up again. "I've had enough of this, Dagger. Who the hell do you think you are, the police? When the *real* police get here, they're going to hear about *you*!" With that, he turned away.

Dagger didn't watch him go. To Mr. Mozamba, he said, "I'm in cabin thirteen if Captain Lumumba wants to talk to me."

Roxanne, the colonel, and I headed back to our quarters and bed. Richard remained, faced the opposite way.

DAGGER AND I were aroused by one of the porters at half past two. "You're wanted up at the lodge," his voice sounded through the louvred doors when we acknowledged the knocking. When we rolled out into the dark of the African night onto the dimly illuminated path, we found Roxanne emerging from the quarters next door. "Not a very good morning," she greeted us.

"They want you, too?"

"Everybody who's seen the body, so the man said."

CAPTAIN LUMUMBA was a very large and very black African. He wore a green uniform with enough gold braid on the sleeves and shoulders to equip a band, and a chestful of medals above his left breast pocket that ran halfway down to his waist. His visored cap was ornate with scrambled eggs,

sidearms were strapped around his middle, twin guns in twin
holsters, he carried a white swagger stick with a leather
handle and strap, and wore leather boots that gleamed like
mirrors. He was big, he was strong, and he was proud.

With him in the lounge were the manager, two of the
lodge's porters, and four armed policemen in khaki uni-
forms. The manager and porters were seated, watching as
Lumumba strode back and forth. The policemen flanked
the doorways at parade rest. Richard, Busby Morgan, and
Duncan Hawley were nowhere in sight.

Captain Lumumba, rocking on his heels, flexing the
swagger stick, studied us in imperious silence as we came in
and positioned ourselves before him. His eye was momen-
tarily attracted to the gold head of the colonel's cane, but
when he spoke, it was to gesture at Dagger with his stick. "I
suppose you're Colonel Dagger." His swagger stick moved
on. "And you're the colonel's daughter, and you're Addison."

We acknowledged his identifications. He left us standing
while he took a brief stroll, staring at the straw rug beneath
his burnished boots. He came back to us. "You were first,
after Hawley, to view the body," he announced. "The three
of you were alone with the body. What did you do and
why?"

The colonel answered. "We checked to make sure he was
dead, discovered that he'd been poisoned by cyanide, re-
ported it to Mr. Mozamba, and locked the room so that no
one could disturb anything."

"Which of you searched the body?"

That stunned me. How the hell did Lumumba know the
body had been searched? Dagger had left the victim and his
possessions exactly as he'd found them. My eyes flickered,
and the captain caught my telltale reaction. On Roxanne's

other side, the colonel answered again, leaning on his cane. "I did," he said smoothly.

"What did you take?"

"Not a thing."

Lumumba's countenance became threatening. "Certain items the deceased was known to be carrying on his person are missing. I ask you *again*. What did you take?"

"Two witnesses will tell you I took nothing."

"Two witnesses who profit by your lie as you profit by it." Lumumba's gaze moved back and forth, looking for another telltale flicker, but this time there was none. "Perhaps you would like to be searched?" he said when no one responded. "Perhaps you would like your baggage searched as well."

"I don't think you'd want to do that, Captain," Dagger answered in that quiet way he had. "The American consulate would get very much upset. They'll be upset enough by an American tourist being murdered on one of your safaris."

Captain Lumumba wandered around, looking at the decorations, the masks, mats, and paintings on the pink stucco walls, whipping his swagger stick against his leg. He came back, his dark eyes savoring us. "Now you will tell me why you three were so quick to go to the body." He fixed his attention on the colonel and pointed with his stick. "You are *not* a doctor. You are *not* a relative. Yet you ran to the body. You would not let others in. You would not even let a doctor in. A rich old man was dead. You wanted to see how much money he had, no?"

"No."

Lumumba kept pointing his stick. Dagger didn't like being pointed at and Lumumba knew it. "*You* ran to the scene."

"I thought I might be able to help."

"A doctor could have helped better, but you did not let the doctor in."

"I found the man to be beyond help."

"So *you* decided. You decide everything. By what authority do you take charge?"

"Habit."

Lumumba blinked. "Habit? What word is habit? What do you mean by habit?"

"Custom, Captain."

Lumumba drew himself up and pointed his swagger stick again. "You will explain yourself. You will explain this *habit*."

"It results from my having been a detective many years ago. I'm sure you know from your own experience that such people go forward instead of backward when there's trouble."

"You were a detective? You can prove this?" Lumumba asked suspiciously.

"I don't use it anymore, but I still carry a license." Dagger took out his wallet, showed Captain Lumumba a card, and replaced it.

Lumumba was silent for a moment. Then he took another little stroll, holding his swagger stick behind his back, this time his gaze studying the ceiling. He planted his feet, his back to us, and said to the ceiling. "What did you find when you searched the body?"

"The usual items," the colonel answered. "Wallet, keys, handkerchief, change. And an unsigned note written by a woman, stating it was imperative that she see him."

Lumumba rocked back and forth, flexing the swagger stick. "How do you know it was a woman?"

"The handwriting looks like a woman's."

"What's the name of the woman?"

"I don't know, but it would be one in the Cartwright Company tour group."

Lumumba snorted. His back was still to us. "What makes you think that?"

"Her request. She thinks he can help her."

"I have had that note shown to every woman on your safari trip. They all deny having written it."

"Then I must be mistaken."

Lumumba didn't like the implied condescension. He turned around slowly. "Africa is for Africans," he said, his voice cold, his eyes like steel. "White-skinned mutants should stay behind their own borders and kill themselves off in their endless wars. They bring us, in Africa, nothing but trouble." He waved us away with his swagger stick. "Go to bed. I've had my fill of white people for tonight. I've never met one yet who wasn't a liar."

WE WENT BACK DOWN the path, and the air bore a distinct morning chill. Roxanne said, "I wonder how long we're going to be held here."

I said, "Probably until Captain Lumumba finds out where the cyanide came from."

"That's what I'm afraid of. Papa," she said to Dagger, "why don't you offer to help him?"

The colonel gave a short laugh. "After his Declaration of Black Supremacy?"

"What I can't figure out," I said, "is how he could tell the body had been searched."

"He couldn't," Dagger answered. "He only set that out as a trap."

I flushed, for I was the one Lumumba's trap had caught. I blundered on. "And how does he know some of Phineas's things were removed?"

Dagger shook his head. "He's guessing. That's another trap."

"How do you know that?" Roxanne asked.

"Because if something really *were* missing, he'd have had us searched."

ELEVEN

Monday, June 23

COLONEL DAGGER slept soundly, but I stopped trying and got up with the sunrise at quarter of seven and put on my clothes. Outside, damned it I didn't find Lise Smith and Busby Morgan pointing out birds to the Kirbys, the Baldwins, Sidney Leggett, and, despite what had happened, Marshall and Sylvia Benedict. All had heard of Phineas's death but none, not even Marshall, whose career was affected by the tragedy, was letting that stand in the way of seeing Africa's birds.

"What's going to happen?" I asked Busby. "About the safari?"

"Captain Lumumba's letting it proceed," Busby answered. "He phoned a report to his superiors in Nairobi, the gist of which, I gather, was that one of the staff members at the lodge brought Phineas a bottle of poisoned liquor, and that none of the guests are involved. Nairobi insisted that the tour group proceed without interruption."

Mary Ellen Baldwin said, "That Phineas! What a dreadful man. Not that I'd've wished anything like *that* on him, but if anyone had to be poisoned, thank goodness it was he."

"At least we'll have peace and quiet," her husband, Harry, answered. "He asked for it, the way he threw his weight around."

"Now if we could just get rid of Richard, too," June noted. "There's always one in every crowd."

"Except," reminded her husband, "in this crowd, there were *two*!"

Lise Smith pointed out a wire-tailed swallow atop a twig on a distant tree. Leggett, the Kirbys, and the Baldwins raised their binoculars. I asked Busby what had been done about Phineas.

He aimed his own binoculars and said, "There it goes," as it flew away. "We're going to have to make some changes," he answered, lowering his glasses, "which I'll announce at breakfast. One of the vans is taking the body back to Nairobi. Richard and Samantha are going with it, of course, to ship it back to the States. So the rest of us will divide among three vans and go on to Kokorok Lodge as scheduled."

THE TRIP TO KOKOROK WAS, for me, out of the frying pan into the fire. If Dagger, Roxanne, and I were rid of Richard and Samantha Cartwright, we took on, as replacements, those two predatory bachelors, Peter Tower and Neville Street, and, in addition, Cartwright Company's wan, lusterless bookkeeper, Jennifer Long.

Peter and Neville outdid each other bidding for Roxanne's favors, a fact she thoroughly enjoyed. They wouldn't let her sit up front with Amram this day, but crowded her between them in the rear seat, nor did she raise the slightest objection. She was loving it. That left Amram alone in front, Dagger and me behind, and Jennifer by herself in the middle passenger seat.

The talk, at first, was solely of Phineas's death. How could anyone at the lodge have poisoned the old man? What kind of retribution was that, just because he was finicky and crotchety? Why would Americans come to Kenya hereafter if that's the way the Kenyans treated them? It was conversation Dagger and I steered clear of, and we were glad no-

body quite dared wonder about the feeling of Kenyans for
Americans, what with Amram up front driving. He seemed
to harbor no ill feeling against us American tourists, but I
couldn't help reflecting upon Captain Lumumba's contempt for white-skinned people from whatever country.

Ultimately, relief was expressed that the dastardly crime
was behind us and we should enjoy our surroundings and
the wonderful experience on an African safari. Dagger had
been silent throughout, holding the cane upright between his
legs, his eyes roving the landscape.

In the rear seat, Peter Tower was now charming Roxanne
with talk about Paris and London. What he could show her,
if she and he could meet in France or England. He was
making great headway against poor Neville, for Neville was
forced to confess this safari was his first trip abroad. Roxanne was joyful and full of laughter and allowed as how
she'd love to have Peter point out the glories of Europe to
her. It almost sounded as if they were making a date.

I darted glances at Dagger. He pretended he wasn't smol-
dering. He even pulled out a notebook and jotted down
names of the birds Amram pointed out as we passed.

Birds weren't my specialty. Roxanne was. But she had me
so totally off balance I didn't know how to approach her.
One thing: I was damned if I was going to jump into the fray
and contend against Peter and Neville for a place in the sun.

Meanwhile, there was lone Jennifer. She'd known Peter
and Neville from way back and I felt sorry for her, being
ignored while they made their pitch to the beauteous newcomer. Dagger seemed to be nodding so I moved into the
seat beside her and started a conversation.

She'd been with Cartwright fourteen years, Jennifer said
in answer to my question. It was the only job she'd held
since she'd finished her training. She was bright and quick
with answers, and all the while she talked, she pretended to

be rapt in the adventure, eyes fixed on the landscape, a notebook open on her lap wherein to record whatever bird Amram pointed out and the time of the sighting. But she wasn't all that clever. I knew her ear was cocked to the bubbling three-way conversation in the seat behind her.

"You know Peter and Neville well?" I wanted to break through her wall.

Her reply was low, the tone flat. "Well enough not to be surprised at the way the two of them chase after a pretty face." She couldn't resist a jibe at herself. "Some women have all the luck. If you're born ugly, like me, it's a totally different world. You don't get to have the fun she's having."

"You aren't ugly."

She turned to me, her plain features alive with bitterness. "Look, you don't have to pretend around me, and you don't have to be polite. I know what I am and there's no point in denying it."

"You do yourself an injustice."

"Do I! You want to know something? I once went to a singles bar. That's right, a singles bar. Don't be shocked. You may think I'm not the type, but you'd be surprised.

"I went there to get picked up. That's right, picked up!

"Now, you'd think *any* girl who wanted to get picked up could get picked up in a singles bar, wouldn't you? But not me. Not ugly little over-thirty Jennifer Long! That whole evening not *one* man said a word to me, paid any attention to me. Not even the bartender, except when I ordered another drink.

"That says something, doesn't it?" She laughed too loudly. "The lady's willing but the gentlemen aren't! How rock bottom can you get? Needless to say, I never went back. I don't need to get hit with a lead pipe to get the message."

There was a rasp in her voice. "That's a pretty funny story, isn't it? Talk about *ugly*! I'm the only woman in the world who could walk naked into a men's locker room and have them all look the other way."

I didn't really want to hear that sort of thing, and from the next time Amram pointed out a bird I kept the conversation limited to the sights we saw.

NOR WERE THEY all birds. Distant animals were in view as well: topi, ostrich, cape buffalo, giraffe. And Amram drove us across fields to a high riverbank so we could get out and see hippos. The other vans pulled up alongside and we stretched our legs for fifteen minutes.

"Stay up on top here," Busby warned, not wanting anyone clambering down to the water's edge. "See the crocodile sunning himself up at the bend?"

Roxanne, well flanked by her admirers, made proper exclamations about the hippos, submerged except for their eyes and snouts, and she *adored* the distant crocodile. I wished her father would take after her suitors as Ulysses went after Penelope's. But Dagger was borrowing Jennifer's notebook to copy names of birds he'd missed. He seemed more damned interested in the grazers and birds of Africa than in the wolves who were pursuing his daughter.

Once under way again (I back with Dagger—no more Jennifer, thank you), driving by miles and miles of head-high dry brown grass, the colonel meticulously noted Amram's explanation that the grass wasn't being eaten because it was too tall. It could hide lions and the grazers wouldn't touch it until the herds of huge wildebeests migrated through and cropped it down to a safe height.

We reached Kokorok Lodge, our stopping place for the next two nights, at half past twelve. This time there was no Phineas or Richard to quarrel about the reservations. We enjoyed lunch, a rest period, an afternoon game drive, which included pulling up alongside a sleeping lioness lying under a tree by herself. Roxanne leaned from the raised roof van top to snap a dozen pictures. Neville, who couldn't compete with Peter's European experiences, suggested he pose with a foot on the lioness and beat his chest, à la Tarzan. Amram didn't bother to comment.

THE FIRST TROUBLE with Kokorok was that baboons appeared at the conjunction of dusk and dinner, and they loped all over the grounds, climbing the roofs, grabbing garbage scraps, and stealing whatever tourist equipment, from cigarettes to cameras, they could seize.

I'd seen their teeth at the baboon park and remembered Gelston's warning of their strength and wildness. At Kokorok, we got further warning: lock your door. Baboons know how to twist knobs, and if they get into your room it's hurricane time.

There was a second trouble at Kokorok which Dagger, Roxanne, and I discovered at dinner. *Richard and Samantha Cartwright were back!*

We'd expected them to take Phineas's body home for burial and no longer embarrass us. But there they were, arriving for dinner, their sullen mutual hatred showing through their attempts at "togetherness."

Peter and Neville were at our table when the two wretched Cartwrights reappeared, and damned if Dagger didn't invite them to join us. They welcomed the colonel's warm approach like manna from heaven and the seven of us ate together.

AT LEAST it put a damper on the rush the two bachelors were giving Roxanne. Everything immediately became formal and conversation descended to poor Phineas and what had happened to bring Richard and Samantha back.

"This safari," Richard explained to us, "was my father's idea. We talked about it, Samantha and I, and we feel he'd want us to go through with it." Samantha nodded agreement. "What is the old saying?" Richard added with an attempt at jocularity, "'The show must go on'?"

Phineas's body was being shipped home for burial, Richard explained—before dismissing the matter as improper dinner conversation—and a memorial service in his honor would be arranged as soon as the safari troop got back. "After all, those of the company who were on the African trip would want the chance to attend."

TWELVE

A NATURE MOVIE on hippos was shown in the lounge after dinner, which everyone, including Richard and Samantha, attended. I hoped Roxanne, Dagger, and I might have a nightcap together afterward, but Neville had preempted her for a drink alone. I wondered at Neville's success, for I was granting Peter, with his "come see the sights of Europe with me" line, the upper hand. But Neville appeared to have effective moves of his own, for he not only had signed Roxanne up for the postmovie drink, but he sat with her throughout the film.

As for the movie, it talked about the two hundred pounds of vegetation a hippo consumed on land during the nighttime hours and how the hippo retreated back to the water come dawn to rest and keep cool, and how the waste material he discharged into the waters produced the nutrients upon which all manner of other species of water creatures thrived.

"One thing," the commentator warned near the end. "Hippos are reasonably harmless. But don't ever get between them and the water. They'll bite you in two with one snap of their jaws if they think you're blocking their access to the water."

When the lights came on, Busby Morgan moved to the front of the room. "One moment," he said, stopping the audience in the midst of rising. "I have an important announcement to make." He gestured for quiet. "We suffered a terrible tragedy last night at Masai Mara Lodge. We suffered the loss of one of our valued safari members. Phineas Cartwright was killed by a bottle of poisoned liqueur. I know there's been a question in all of our minds as to who could have done such a terrible thing. I'm able to report to you now that the guilty person has been found. It was a waiter at the lodge.'' Busby opened a slip of paper. ''I have his name here, but I can't pronounce it. But I have learned through Captain Lumumba's office that the young man has confessed. While this was a terrible thing to have happen to one of our group, I know all of us can breathe easier knowing that the criminal has been arrested and that justice in Kenya is like justice in the United States. We grieve for the loss of Phineas Cartwright, one of the outstanding members of our group, but we applaud the Kenyan police for their quick, effective solution of the case.''

Some hand-clapping followed, but an undercurrent of hisses erupted as well, probably for Busby's gratuitous remarks about Phineas's importance to the group.

THAT ENDED THE EVENING as far as I was concerned. It was the same for Dagger, and we returned to our quarters together, but we didn't speak. I was full of questions: how did Dagger think Lumumba had solved the case? Why would a waiter, no matter how upset, poison a guest, and where would he get the poison?

And, much more to the point: why did Dagger invite Richard and Samantha to join our table for dinner? What did he think of Neville's beating Peter Tower out with Roxanne this evening? Would it be permanent? How much did Dagger think Roxanne cared about either Peter or Neville?

But Dagger was preoccupied and disturbed, and best left alone. He went to bed with no more than a grunted ''Good night.''

I DON'T KNOW what woke me, but the night was dark. A
faint yellow glow from the walkway lights came through our
windows, which opened onto a tiny concrete slab of porch
and looked across the plains toward where, less than a mile
away, we'd come across the sleeping lioness.

I sensed something was amiss, but didn't know what. I
pushed the button that lighted my digital wristwatch and the
time was half past four. As my eyes grew accustomed to the
dimness, I could make out that Colonel Dagger's bed was
empty, the covers cast back. I assumed he was in the bathroom, but realized its door was open and there was no light.

I sat up. The colonel wasn't in the room. Uneasiness filled
me. It wasn't that he couldn't take care of himself, but I
suddenly remembered Roxanne's warning that he was not
well, that he needed help. He wouldn't let her stay with him,
and she'd put the responsibility upon me.

I rose and groped my way around his bed. His clothes
were gone from the chair where he'd left them, and I became aware of the strong smell of cigarette smoke. He
couldn't be far. I looked out the door.

He was there, on the patch of porch, in the one chair beside a small wicker table. His omnipresent cane was propped
against the chair, pinned to the arm by his thigh. On the table was an ashtray full of stubs, a pack of cigarettes, two
packets of matches, a tumbler from the bathroom, and a
nearly empty bottle of Scotch. He saw me and he grunted.
The cigarette in his fingers was down to the filter and he
turned to mash it out, helping himself to another at the same
time. "I didn't mean to disturb you," he said in a thick,
heavy voice. "Sometimes I have trouble sleeping."

"You didn't disturb me," I assured him. "Are you all
right?"

"I'm all right," he answered, and looked for a moment
across the flat land into the darkness. He took a drag on the

new cigarette that would knock out a horse and turned to the glass and bottle. "Would you care for a drink?" He tilted the bottle to gauge its contents. "There's a little left." He put down the cigarette and picked up the glass.

"No, thank you."

"I hope you don't mind if I have one?" He poured the balance of the Scotch into the tumbler, an inch's worth, set the bottle down, and half emptied the glass with one sip. He retrieved the cigarette with the other hand and took another ferocious drag. Smoke must have leaked out of his toes.

I regarded him uncertainly. Until this moment, I'd never seen him with a cigarette. And the liquor he'd drunk! All he'd done before was take occasional sips of a light Scotch and soda. Now he'd emptied a liter bottle of Scotch, drinking it straight. I wondered that he could light a cigarette or hold a glass. I wondered that he could speak coherently. He was showing the effects, to be sure. He was moody, his head tilted forward so that his chin nearly rested on his chest. His voice was thick and hoarse, his thinking slowed, but through it all he seemed to know exactly what he was doing, exactly what it was doing to him, and that that was exactly what he was after.

Roxanne had said he suffered pain. She feared he was alcoholic. I didn't know. Maybe chain-smoking cigarettes and putting away a liter of Scotch was his way of handling bad nights. If so, I was glad I didn't have nights like that. But we all have our own way of dealing with our own problems and that was his business. He wouldn't let Roxanne monitor him, he certainly wouldn't want to hear anything from me.

"You know, it's stupid," he said out of nowhere, as I was about to go back inside. He took his cane and rapped its tip against the concrete floor. "It's so stupid."

"What is?" I stayed where I was.

He sat slumped in the chair now, head bowed, eyes watching the tip of the cane as it bounced against the concrete.

"I wonder," he went on, "what the kid's name is—the one Busby Morgan couldn't pronounce. I wonder about his family."

"You mean the waiter who poisoned Phineas?"

He rose a little, scowling. "No waiter poisoned Phineas," he said, marshaling himself, sitting higher. "No Kenyan poisoned Phineas. Phineas was poisoned by someone in our own group. One of those people in the Cartwright Company."

My jaw dropped. Despite the bottle of Scotch, until that statement I'd thought him remarkably sober. "Well, now," I said placatingly, "I don't think Captain Lumumba would make a mistake about such a thing. I think he'd much rather pin the crime on a white tourist than one of his own countrymen. Besides, Busby told us the culprit confessed."

"So did Galileo 'confess.' So have any number of other people confessed: little people who didn't enjoy Galileo's reputation."

My eyes widened. "You think Lumumba and his crew beat a confession out of an innocent waiter? But why?"

Dagger shook his head slowly, paid enough heed to the fact he held a cigarette to take another earth-shaking drag, and emptied the balance of his Scotch before exhaling. "Who knows what they did? Maybe they believed the kid was guilty. Maybe they can't imagine a tourist committing murder on foreign soil. Maybe it's tourism. It's a Kenyan staple and they don't want it disturbed." He pushed himself to his feet, leaning heavily on the cane. "But we can't have that, James. We've got a murderer in our midst. We can't let it just lie there. Something has to be done."

I was staggered. "You're saying it's someone in the Cart-wright group? How can you know that?"

He didn't answer. "I think I'll go for a walk," he said, and moved off the porch onto the grass, starting in the direction of the lodge. He was trying to hide the pain, but for the first time his limp was noticeable. So was his stagger.

There was nothing for me except return to bed. But I was still awake a half hour later when Dagger returned, undressed, and climbed silently into his own bed.

THIRTEEN

Tuesday, June 24

I THOUGHT Colonel Dagger would sleep in and skip the morning game drive, something I would have done myself except for missing Roxanne. But no, he rose at a knock on the door shortly before seven, when the sun was just up, and went in to shower without a trace of fatigue, or a limp, or a night full of booze. I had to push my eyelids open, but he was as fresh as the bright new day.

Outside, when we went to breakfast, two gaily colored hot-air balloons were drifting over the landscape. For two hundred dollars, we'd been told, a dozen people could float above the fields and forests viewing animals from the air, landing for a champagne breakfast out on the plains, and return to Kokorok for lunch. That was what Richard and Samantha did; what Roxanne, Dagger and I did *not* do, and we three had the van and Amram to ourselves for a visit to herds of elephants who chewed on trees and paid us little attention. It was the most pleasant morning I'd had in a week.

The afternoon drive, which was highlighted by discreetly distant views of cape buffalo (they're the meanest animals in Africa, Amram told us, and would charge if we got within range), was something else again. Richard and Samantha had rejoined us and the tension was palpable. Dagger pretended not to notice and resolutely questioned them about their morning. Who else had gone on the balloon ride, he inquired.

"The Benedicts and the Gambles," Richard told him, "and Duncan Hawley." The Gambles, the Cartwrights, and Hawley, it seemed, had shared the same balloon. The Benedicts were in the other one.

"I wonder who paid Hawley's way?" Richard sneered at the end. "He's so tight he's still wearing the first suit of clothes he ever bought."

"He certainly wouldn't get his way paid by *you*," Samantha retorted. "The last time you put a dime in a blind man's cup, your mother had to lift you up."

"Guess who was scared up in the balloon," Richard taunted back. "The great female athlete and golfer." To Samantha, he scoffed, "You should have had a mirror up there. That beautiful tan you're so proud of was the color of cigar ash."

But Samantha could drive her own nails. "It's a good thing Duncan came along," she retorted. "You *should* have paid his way. The way you were trying to paw Harriet Gamble in that tiny basket, if he hadn't been in between, George would have broken your jaw."

"Too bad George wasn't interested in pawing *you*. I don't know what it is you lack."

That was the kind of dialogue we had to endure when we started out. Dagger seemed interested to the point of encouraging them, but I find it painful listening to couples bicker in public. Fortunately, after Amram pointed out a bateleur eagle and a gray hornbill, and we saw a hyena suckling her cubs at her nest hole, the Cartwrights quieted down.

On our way back from the cape buffalo, we came upon a couple of male lions lying under a bush. We parked within ten feet of them but they ignored us and the nearer one acted as if dead. Amram said lions sometimes use that "dead act" as a ploy.

WEDNESDAY, WE BROKE CAMP in the morning and the four
vans took a game drive en route to our next stop, a place cut
out of the jungle called Coulter's Camp. There we were assigned to rustic cabins connected by a trail and scattered
through the woods. Wash water, as at Kokorok, was
warmed by solar heat and when the sun went down, the water cooled. Showers at midnight at Coulter would be cold.
Also the temperature. Eight of the party, including the Kirbys and Baldwins, Roxanne, the colonel, Neville Street, and
me, signed up for a night game drive, which was a mistake.
We piled into the rear of a large passenger truck and drove
through the frigid blackness for three fruitless hours while
the boy on top of the cab beamed his searchlight at empty
fields. Keeping us out an extra hour to try to show us *something* only made us colder. When we got back at midnight,
there was no hot water and I was a long time under heavy
blankets getting warm again.

As I reflected at this point, huddled under the covers, the
rest of the group seemed totally to have forgotten that
Phineas Cartwright had ever existed. Even Samantha and
Richard hadn't mentioned his name since their return report. Nor had Dagger said a word since finishing off that
bottle of Scotch on our little porch at Kokorok at five
o'clock in the morning.

But what he'd said kept haunting me: that Phineas hadn't
been killed by a Kenyan waiter, he'd been poisoned by
someone in our own group, someone from the Cartwright
Company! Everyone else was enjoying the safari, but all I
could do was keep sifting through the names of the Cartwright members, giving them all suspicious stares.

I sorted through them once again to forget the cold:
Richard and Samantha Cartwright; Marshall and Sylvia
Benedict; George and Harriet Gamble; Duncan Hawley;
Lucy Children; Jennifer Long; Peter Tower and Neville

Street. They were all ordinary, unexceptional human beings, totally unsuited for murder. What would any of them want to kill Phineas for, especially in a strange land on a safari trip?

The only answer, I decided, was that Captain Lumumba had solved the case and Colonel Dagger's alternative theory stemmed from a liter of Scotch and resentment at Lumumba's contempt for a man who'd been a king in his day, a top-flight detective, a superb novelist, a richly successful screenwriter.

I only wished Dagger would tell me that himself and set my mind at ease.

FOURTEEN

Thursday, June 26

A LONG DRIVE lay ahead for us the next morning, from Coulter's Camp, back through Narok to the A104, turning west to Lake Naivasha, instead of east to Nairobi.

We hit the Narok pit and rest stop at 11:00 and when I disembarked to stretch my legs, I did a double take. There, wandering among the gas pumps, clapping an authoritative black hand on the white sides of our vans, was the towering, bemedaled figure of Captain Lumumba, Narok's key police power!

He seemed jovial and gregarious, chatting with the drivers in Swahili, the tourists in English, but his reappearance gave me a chill. I knew his hatred of whites and what we stood for and I'd hoped never to see him again.

Roxanne was equally amazed. So were the other safari members. I queried Dagger as to what it could mean, but he only shrugged with an "I'm a stranger here myself" attitude. Nevertheless, though the rest of us were chagrined at Lumumba's presence, I detected a hint of pleasure underneath Dagger's casual manner.

"I don't understand your father," I whispered to Roxanne. "He hates that Captain Lumumba, yet he seems glad to see him back."

Roxanne patted my arm. "Don't try to understand Papa," she murmured into my ear. "He quit detecting, he quit screenwriting, he's quit three wives. He prefers solitude and pain. Accept him. Don't try to psychoanalyze him. It's impossible."

THE REEMERGENCE of such a formidable figure as Captain Lumumba did not pass unresented, even as he went cheerily among us tourists, greeting us as long lost friends. We knew he wasn't there to wave us on. Even before he made the announcement, we were aware he was there to become a part of our lives.

"Your attention, please," he smiled, speaking his rich baritone English, waving us close when we gathered to reboard our vans. "Narok welcomes the American tourists. I, personally, must profess my deepest sorrow at the death of one of your members. Such a happening reflects upon the reputation of the government of Kenya. My government is greatly concerned that nothing like this ever happens again."

He gestured with a wave that, somehow, caused all his medals and ribbons to gleam in the sunlight. "The government of Kenya," he continued, "has assigned me the high honor of protecting you from further mishap. It is my pleasure to be privileged to accompany and guard your group throughout the rest of its stay."

With that announcement, he swung into the front seat of Amram's van and looked around with a beaming smile as the rest of us boarded our respective conveyances and a carful of his men got ready to follow. Richard and Samantha, having to share our van with the unpopular captain, were understandably sullen. Roxanne had question marks in her eyes. My own eyes projected anger. And Dagger! Damned if he didn't seem pleased the monster had chosen to ride with us!

Lumumba talked with Amram in their own language, but though I didn't understand, I well knew what he was telling

Amram wasn't what he was telling us passengers. With us he was exceedingly politic and exceedingly vague, traits that did not become him any more than smiles and jocularity.

Richard bedeviled him with questions. Richard wanted to know why Lumumba thought we needed protection, hadn't he already arrested the waiter who'd poisoned his father? What other Kenyans did Lumumba think wanted to do us harm? Why would any beneficiaries of American tourism bite the hand that fed them? Why would any self-respecting American want to come to this godforsaken country to look at animals anyway?

Lumumba remained unruffled and sidestepped direct answers with such fudgings as "government policy," "friendship with America," "mutual protection treaties," until my teeth were on edge. I wished I could force the truth out of him but knew no one could succeed at that except Colonel Dagger. Only Dagger could match Lumumba in expertise and know-how.

But Dagger was playing his own game. He was more interested in the offerings of a curio shop we stopped at en route, though he bought nothing. Dagger was more interested in the dead hartebeest we drove over the fields to find lying under a high-flying, slowly descending circle of white-backed vultures. I fancied myself enough of a detective to realize he was deliberately giving Lumumba full rein and reign.

THE HOTEL NAIVASHA, at the side of the lake, was typical nineteenth-century British colonial. It was a low, rambling, white-framed building with broad sweeping lawns, as closely cropped as a fairway and dotted with tea tables, stretching down to the lake shore, with residential duplex dwellings strung along the sides to house the guests.

We arrived at half past one to a sumptuous lunch, and a number of us boarded dories at four for an hour's cruise over the lake waters, viewing wallowing hippopotami, watching pelicans run across the surface to get airborne, taking pictures of cormorant "apartment houses" in the dead trees, killed by the spreading of the lake, that rose like ghostly fingers out of the water.

The dories carried eight passengers, and the inescapable Captain Lumumba was in *our* boat, along with the Gambles and Benedicts. At least he spoke little. He hunched uneasily in the middle seat, as if afraid of the water. The snorts of the hippos caused him unease, and the way pelicans gain flying speed left him unmoved. I could not but conclude he was on assignment and that the assignment was not to his liking.

We disembarked at five, and Neville Street, riding in the next boat, hurried to Roxanne for a quick, whispered conference. I wanted to eavesdrop but Lumumba, once back on land, towering and in full swagger again, planted himself beside me on the walk back to the hotel.

"This is your first trip to Kenya, Mr. Addison?"

"Yes, it is."

"I hope you understand, think what you will of me, that I have a job to do?"

How I wanted to tell him *exactly* what I thought of him and ask just what that job was! I said, instead, "I can understand that. We all have jobs to do." But I couldn't help adding, "Even in the United States."

"Yes," he answered. "We all. According to our lights."

"And your lights, Captain?"

"Kenya. As yours are the United States of America."

"So far we understand each other."

"Your Colonel Dagger? He is a famous detective?"

"Well known," I said, defending him as best I could. "I don't know that he's *famous*."

"But you room with him?"

"On this trip, yes."

"Does he still practice detecting?"

"Sir," I said, stopping to face the captain, "I don't know. You should ask him."

"And I will," Captain Lumumba answered. "Tell me something. I'm much interested in detecting. I do a little of it myself. Does the colonel sleep well at night?"

"Again, you should ask him."

"True," Lumumba smiled. "I could, indeed, ask him. But I'm asking you. You room with him. Is he restless at night? Does he pace the floor? Is he awake at all hours? So many people like him are."

"I'm sure," I said, still facing him, "I couldn't tell you. That's a question only the colonel can answer. I'm sure, if you put it to him, he'll tell you."

I got away from Captain Lumumba then, and headed back to the hotel.

FIFTEEN

Thursday, June 26

I TOLD DAGGER about Lumumba's questioning over a Scotch and soda on the lawn. Roxanne was having cocktails with Neville Street at another table, and the rest of the group, including Captain Lumumba, were sipping tea under nearby trees listening to Lise Smith talk about and point out the birds of the area. The only birds I noticed were the storks who flew overhead at treetop level with a great whir of wings.

I expected Dagger to be amused at Lumumba's interest in his sleeping habits. Instead, he was angered. "That's *not* what he's supposed to be here for," the colonel exploded, looking deep into the heart of his Scotch and soda glass.

"You know what he's supposed to be here for?"

Dagger downed the rest of his drink, signaled a passing waiter for a triple, and pulled out an unopened pack of cigarettes, quickly lighting and inhaling one. The inhale of smoke to the depths of his lungs seemed to steady him. "I know what he *ought* to be here for," he answered.

"Which is what?"

"To find out who killed Phineas Cartwright." Dagger was sullen about it. "Why else?"

"But I thought he knew."

"He doesn't know. Nobody knows. That's why he's back. At least, that's why he's *supposed* to be back. If it's not that, God only knows the real reason."

I was baffled, but I groped. "This has to do with your saying the man who killed Phineas wasn't the waiter, but somebody in the Cartwright group?"

Dagger didn't even deign to nod. "Not *man*, *person*. It could be a woman. But it wasn't any Kenyan waiter. As I told you before—perhaps you didn't believe me because I was in my cups." He waved a careless hand. "Ignore that. I'm in my cups a good part of the time. In Hollywood, I was in my cups all the time. My then wife and I drank twenty-four hours a day. We lived on booze. She lived on drugs as well." He gestured again with that careless hand. "But that's a long time past. To get back, as I told you before, someone in the Cartwright group poisoned Phineas. And please don't ask me how I know. The answer is too obvious. The bar at the Masai Mara doesn't carry Père Javineau liqueur. I checked. So it had to be brought from Nairobi. The card—'Compliments of the Holcomb Travel Agency'—had to come from Nairobi, too. You can pick them up at the Nairobi Sabrina Hotel, but not at the Masai Mara. The waiter was a pawn. Someone phoned the desk to have the poisoned bottle and Holcomb card delivered to Phineas. It was done, and Phineas died, and the poor waiter is being blamed."

Dagger stamped his cane upon the grass. "It won't do, James. We can't let that sort of thing happen."

"But what would bring Lumumba back?" I queried. "I don't believe his false enthusiasm and his insistence that he's only here to ride 'shotgun.' That doesn't make any sense. On the other hand, he claimed he'd caught the murderer, and we all believed him—except you, Colonel. So why's he back, riding with us, questioning me about you, questioning other people about God-knows what? That's not the attitude of a bodyguard. It sounds as if he *himself* isn't so sure anymore that the 'butler done it.'" I sipped my drink and

watched one of the storks flap by overhead. Thirty yards
away, at tables under stately trees, Captain Lumumba, the
black of his skin, the gold and green of his uniform, and his
restless swagger stick making him as eye-catching as the
moon at night, sat with the bird watchers listening atten-
tively to tall, slender, blond Lise. "I wonder," I said, viewing him briefly, "what could have changed his mind."

"*I* did!" Dagger answered abruptly. "That is, if his mind
actually is changed."

"You?" I stared at the relaxed, long-legged man in the
chair beside me. "How? When?"

The colonel took a drag that finished his cigarette and
crushed it in the glass tray. "I phoned in an anonymous tip
to the police. The time was five o'clock in the morning,
which wasn't the best time, but it might have added cre-
dence. At least we have Captain Lumumba with us again,
and he's doing detecting, but, from what you tell me, it
seems to be directed toward finding out who phoned in the
anonymous tip instead of who killed Phineas Cartwright."

"You phoned from Kokorok! When you went for a
'walk'!"

"That was when I got the idea."

I was amazed. "You called to get him to reopen the case?
What did you tell him?"

"I didn't call Narok. I called his superiors in Nairobi."
Dagger paused to sign the chit when our waiter set three
jiggers of Scotch, three glasses of ice cubes, and three small
bottles of soda in front of him. He offered me one of the
Scotches and when I declined, poured all three into his own
glass. "There's nothing like a word from superiors," he
continued, "to fill a man's soul with ambition. To phone a
tip to Lumumba himself would be like dropping a pebble in
a well."

"What did you say to them?"

Dagger usually drank small amounts of Scotch in large amounts of soda and ice. At this moment, he didn't bother with soda and ice, but sipped his Scotch straight, and I wondered if he were settling in for another long, hard night with the bottle. "I said," he answered, "that I was going to give them an anonymous tip about the murder of the American tourist at the Masai Mara Lodge. I said the poisoned liqueur had been purchased in Nairobi by a member of the Cartwright Company tourists, a person whose name I was not permitted to disclose. I said it was a rare liqueur which was Phineas Cartwright's favorite and the killer knew this when he bought it."

I laughed at his boldness. Boldness helps in article writing, too, but the colonel's exceeded mine. "Good God," I said. "What was their response?"

"I detected quite a bit of choking. Also, a good deal of trying to find out who I was, and who the real murderer was."

"And you wouldn't tell them?"

"I don't know who the real murderer is. I only know it isn't that young Kenyan waiter they'd forced to confess."

"But how did you know that Père Javineau liqueur was Phineas's favorite?"

"I don't. I just said that to stir up some action." Dagger shook a fresh cigarette loose from the pack, plucked it up, studied it, snarled in angry rejection, and returned it. "I have to suspect," he went on, "Lumumba was convinced the murderer was a local man only because he couldn't imagine a tourist bringing in cyanide. Such a tourist, if caught, would be hard put to explain himself—or herself. I had to get him past that mental block."

Lise Smith's lecture on birds broke up. The safari members wandered off toward their quarters and Captain Lumumba came our way, striking his stick against his leg, always a sign of displeasure. "You aren't interested in African birdlife?" he challenged when he reached us, his eyes cold and unremitting.

Dagger waved at a chair. "Sit down, Captain. Would you care for a drink?"

The captain sat, but he braced his hands on the table, his swagger stick between them. "No drink," he said. "I repeat. You do not like African birdlife?"

The hand that held the glass of Scotch became remarkably still. "African birdlife is beautiful," Dagger replied in his especially quiet voice. "What I don't like is being challenged."

"What *I* don't like," Lumumba countered, "are people who mind other people's business."

Dagger raised his glass to him. "We understand each other."

"Does that mean you are willingly confessing?"

"Confessing? To what?"

Lumumba took a deep breath and replanted his hands upon the table. "Perhaps, then, I must change my approach. Have you been sleeping well on this safari trip?"

"That's the same question you asked Mr. Addison. Is my ability to sleep important?"

"Perhaps more important is the question, do you walk in your sleep? Do you, perhaps, make telephone calls in your sleep?"

"In Africa?"

"At Kokorok Lodge, for example? Would you, perhaps, have made an early morning call to Nairobi?"

"To Nairobi? To whom in Nairobi? On what subject?"

"I will ask the questions here. You will answer."

"Not without telling me what you're talking about. Not without addressing me in a more appropriate manner."

Their eyes met in a hard gaze. Then Captain Lumumba sneered. "Pah," he said. "Your answers would be useless. I've known many white men in my life, but I've never met one who wasn't a liar."

"A point you've made before." Dagger took a sip of his Scotch. "In which case, as you suggest, no purpose is served by asking me questions."

Lumumba, angered, leaned toward Dagger, putting an elbow on the table. "I'm going to tell you something, Colonel," he said in a voice that would have been deep and rich if it hadn't been so harsh. "But if you want my view, you already know it."

Now he rapped the handle of his swagger stick on the table in rhythm with his words. "New evidence has developed in the murder case involving your Phineas Cartwright, evidence which clears the man who tried to take responsibility for the crime. That means the criminal is still at large." He fixed Dagger with steady eye. "That means he's a member of this safari tour." He paused and waited.

Dagger asked blandly, "Is that what the phone call was about? The one to Nairobi from Kokorok?"

"I think you know the answer better than I," Lumumba answered. "If I did not believe that, I would not be telling you this."

"Now that you have, what's the rest? You're here now to find the real poisoner?"

Lumumba sat back. "What I do and why I do it is no concern of yours. I have responsibilities and I will handle them in my own way and at my own pleasure. Soon I shall have to announce my purpose to the group as a whole. You shall not learn about it until they do."

My attention was distracted by an outcry, and I turned to see several of our tour group hurrying our way. Richard Cartwright, Peter Tower, and Marshall Benedict were has-

tening over the lawns elbow to elbow while an alarmed
Duncan Hawley, emerging from his own cabin, broke into
a half trot to catch up.

"Captain Lumumba," they exclaimed when they reached
us, all but breathless, "this is an outrage."

"What is?" he asked, all innocence.

"Our rooms, our luggage, our clothes, our closets,
everything has been searched!"

I sat up and said to Dagger, "Our room, too, then?"
Dagger remained unmoved.

"Thieves," the four men exclaimed. "Thieves have ran-
sacked our rooms!"

Lumumba was but mildly concerned. "Was anything
taken?"

"We haven't found out yet. We only just discovered it."
The four men gesticulated. "Come and see."

"I'll take your word for it," Lumumba answered, displaying an infuriating disinterest. "Make a list of anything
missing and report it to the hotel manager."

"Hotel manager!" Richard exploded, incensed. "You're
the police! You're the one who's in authority here! I insist
that you take personal charge of the investigation!"

"That would require orders from my superiors in Nairobi," Lumumba answered with total lack of concern.
"Have them order me to comply with your wishes and I
shall certainly do so. Otherwise, the person to complain to
is the hotel manager."

The foursome, cursing Lumumba in futile fury, stalked
off toward the hotel. As for me, I was sufficiently incensed
to beard Lumumba myself. "We know what you think of
white people and it's quite obvious you've had no experience with public relations, but it would seem that a captain
of police would have at least a little concern for the victims

of a crime, no matter what their nationality or the color of their skin.''

His reply was a cold and contemptuous dismissal. ''Only when I'm ordered.''

Then Dagger asked him, ''Did you really think you'd find cyanide in anybody's luggage?''

Lumumba rose and smote the metal table with his swagger stick. ''And you,'' he said, pointing it at Dagger's face, ''are to keep your nose out of this case. You've butted in enough already!''

He turned on his heel and strode away.

SIXTEEN

Thursday-Friday, June 26-27

CAPTAIN LUMUMBA had so alienated the safari group that he was shunned at dinner and ate alone, his smile and charm gone, his scowl and distaste firmly back in place.

The Cartwrights and Gambles were eating together, and when Richard waved us to the two extra chairs, damned if Dagger didn't accept. I got my fill of the Cartwrights on the van rides and was hoping we could horn in on Roxanne and Neville over in the corner by themselves. But Dagger, for whatever reason, smiled at the new Cartwright Company head and led the way.

If I couldn't figure Dagger, I also couldn't figure Richard. From what I'd overheard on the plane, Richard hated George Gamble. Now they were sitting chummily together, their wives on their other sides, and Richard all but had his arm around George. He also had exciting news to tell us. He was moving George Gamble up the corporate ladder. George would hereafter handle all the firm's important legal business himself. George would also become Richard's personal attorney.

George, his squirrel cheeks puffed with smiles, looked like cock of the walk, and Harriet wore a self-satisfied grin. Samantha was the only one who viewed the new arrangement with suspicion. I was with her. George looked completely trusting and I wouldn't have trusted Richard if I had him in handcuffs. Gamble had believed the old man liked him, but Phineas was going to feed him to the wolves when they got home. Gamble equally well believed Richard hated him, yet Richard was acting like his best friend. I was bewildered.

And what about Marshall Benedict? He and Sylvia were at a nearby table with Lucy Children and Jennifer Long, and they couldn't keep their eyes off Richard and his enthusiasm for George Gamble. What was going to happen to *them* when this trip ended?

I looked around for the rest of the Cartwright contingent. How were Duncan Hawley, Peter Tower, and Neville Street taking this obvious show Richard was putting on? Richard was king now, and loving it. Power was suffusing his face with ruddiness. He ordered wine for the table and proposed a toast to George. I spotted Peter and Duncan eating together. Duncan's attention was, as Richard meant it to be, on Richard's table. Peter's attention, on the other hand, was directed toward his plate. As for Neville, he was so bemused by Roxanne, he didn't even know the sun had set.

Colonel Dagger proved as much interested in Richard's plans for George as George was. Dagger was congratulatory and even asked to have his menu autographed in remembrance of the occasion. Samantha, on his left, smiled with her mouth, but not with her eyes, and wrote, "A great evening, a great trip. Fondly." Richard, with a flourish, scribbled, "More power to the Cartwright Company, long may she wave. Best wishes." George's note said, "If you ever come to Cartwright Country, please look us up." Harriet hemmed and hawed, then wrote, "It's been *so* nice knowing you. Such a fun trip!" Dagger passed the card to me last and I couldn't help writing, "This is the best time I've had since cocktails with Lumumba."

He grinned at my message, folded the card, and put it in his pocket instead of showing it around. He was protecting me from myself.

There was more stupid talk about the Cartwright Company and the changes Richard was going to introduce. Not a word was said about dear departed Phineas. He hadn't earned a sobriquet and without that, once you're dead, only the worms care.

I kept sliding glances at Neville Street cozying up to the willing Roxanne, and I knew that Dagger had an eye on them, too. I wondered about Peter Tower, Neville's supposed adversary, whose only glances, when he took his head out of his soup, were toward our table, not Neville's.

So MUCH FOR THE HOTEL at Lake Naivasha. We left at quarter past eight the following morning for Lake Baringo, north of the equator, to see hippopotami. Captain Lumumba rode in van no. 3 this time, with Peter, Neville, Lucy Children, and Jennifer Long. Busby Morgan rode with us, pointing out our first reticulated giraffes.

At Lake Nakura, home for two and a half million flamingos, all vans parked on the hard-packed sand of the beach and we neophytes spent half an hour wandering near the great pink birds, who moved steadfastly away if you got closer than thirty feet. Roxanne strolled over the soda-stained sand snapping pictures, with Neville Street showing her how. Though Roxanne rode with Dagger, the Cartwrights, and me, the moment the vans came to a halt, there was Neville at her elbow, acting like a fifteen-year-old brother taking care of his six-year-old sister. Peter wandered around by himself, scowling, taking sneak glances at the twosome. He didn't like it, but Neville had cut him out.

As for me, I hated Neville Street. It wasn't because he was making the most headway, it was because Roxanne opened

the door to him and kept it closed to me. I wasn't even being
allowed to compete. What was it she'd said about my article on New York City as a bachelor's paradise? Never mind.
She'd read it and she was just *waiting* for me to make a
move!

Richard Cartwright remained in the van. Samantha
jogged around on the beach, saying she was keeping herself
in shape. I looked to see whom she was trying to impress,
but nobody paid any attention except Sidney Leggett, who
didn't want her frightening the birds.

Back in the vans, Busby asked Richard why he didn't get
out to see the flamingos and Richard answered, "What for?
I've seen flamingos at Hialeah."

WE CROSSED the equator at noon, south to north, and
everybody took pictures of everybody at the big yellow sign
beside the road that said, at the top, YOU ARE NOW
CROSSING THE—with the word EQUATOR spelled
across the middle of the African continent painted in black.
Even Richard had his picture taken at that site, he on one
side of the sign, Samantha on the other. Hialeah doesn't
have signs like that.

OUR DESTINATION was the Baringo Lodge on the shores of
hippo-laden Lake Baringo, and we arrived at 1:00 for lunch
and a two-night stay. Beyond the main lodge, a long, paved
path through the middle of the grounds led to tourist quarters spaced in a semicircle 150 yards distant, while a paralleling stone wall separated the close-cropped lawns from the
thick growth of grasses and shrubs that covered the sandy
soil between the lodge and the lake itself, a hundred yards
away.

Baringo Lodge offered a scattering of activities to fill our
afternoon. One could pay for a boat ride on the lake to see

the hippos; there was a native village we could visit where, for a fee, the natives would do their tribal dance, or, close at hand, one could buy a ride on a camel. The camel path, cutting through the lakeshore grasses some fifty feet beyond our wall, offered a twenty-minute trip up and back, the lone camel being led by a small lad of twelve who held the halter and carried a control stick. It was not the smoothest of rides, and it was under the hot African sun, but Roxanne took it. It was the first thing she did after lunch.

I made a point of being at the debarking point when the young lad brought her back. It was hot, dusty, and still and no one else was around. I shot some pictures of the lad settling the camel to its knees and helping Roxanne off its back. It wasn't a lion eating a zebra, but it *was* Africa.

"You've *got* to try it," she said, joining me. "Let me see, I've ridden horses, donkeys, ponies, now I've ridden a camel. I think, like Sidney Leggett, I should keep a life-list. A life-list of things I've ridden."

"Let me see," I said, "the subway, the roller coaster, the merry-go-round. It mounts up."

She told me never to mind, I was being facetious. I said, "Would you like a gin and tonic?"

She looked at her watch. "Well," was her reply, "only if we can make it quick. Neville's taking me to visit the native village and the bus goes in twenty minutes."

SEVENTEEN

I ATTENDED a predinner slide show on birds of Kenya at 7:00 in the lounge but nobody I cared about was there, not Dagger, not Roxanne and Neville, not even Captain Lumumba. Lumumba was at dinner, though, shunned, ignored, and chewing his cud. I ate the roast duck with Dagger, but he was out of sorts himself, quiet and withdrawn. I sensed his eye was on Roxanne and Neville dining chummily in a corner. The Cartwrights ate with the Gambles again, Richard expansive, ordering wine for their table, beaming on George and Harriet, Samantha deliberately ignored and ignoring.

A movie about Africa, called *Seasons in the Sun*, was to be shown in the nearby rec building at 9:15, which I could have done without, but thought I ought to see. To my surprise, Dagger chose to go, too, and we wandered over together. Rows of folding chairs had been set out across the floor in front of the screen and most of the seats were filled. I didn't get a count of everyone who was there, but I guessed those on our tour were on hand.

The movie lasted an hour and when the lights came on, the projectionist hurried forward, clapping his hands and saying, "One moment. Your attention, please," and faced us in front of the screen.

"As you know," he said, "Lake Baringo is the home of hippos. Though they spend their days in the lake, they come ashore at night to feed. You will probably hear them grunting in the marshes. They're not dangerous if you keep your distance, but I must ask you, when you leave here, to stay on the lighted paths and don't wander off into the dark, for they frequently come over the wall and get onto the grounds. So mind that you stay on the paths where the lights are. Are there any questions?''

No hands were lifted, but Captain Lumumba came striding forward, announcing, "I have something to say." He waved the projectionist away and raised his hands for attention. He looked very grim.

"I've tried to be friendly to you all," he announced, his dark eyes searching the room. "We, here in Kenya, are pleased to have you safari tourists as our guests. We like you. We welcome you." The glare in his eyes belied his words.

"I have not wanted to alarm you, my friends. I've tried to ride with you and talk with you in a friendly manner. I've wanted you to believe that my presence was out of concern for you and your safety, which the Kenyan government wants to insure.

"My presence," he went on, "has nevertheless been met with great hostility. If my job has been made difficult, it is *your* fault. If I have to give you bad news, it's not because I want to. *You* have forced me to do it."

He had the attention of his audience all right. There wasn't a sound.

"One of your group," he went on, "Mr. Phineas Cartwright, died drinking poisoned liqueur back at the Masai Mara Lodge. We arrested the man we thought had done it. But we were wrong. New evidence proved him innocent. It is my duty to find the guilty party. This is why I am with you. This is why I've been asking questions."

He scowled fearfully. "You people have not been ready with answers. You've made it difficult for me. But I will be *frank* with you. Mr. Cartwright was poisoned by a bottle of

Père Javineau liqueur. That liqueur, which was his favorite, was not to be found on the shelves of the Masai Mara Lodge. That bottle was brought to the lodge by his murderer. And his murderer is someone right here in this room."

With the shock waves still reverberating, Captain Lumumba produced a folded paper. "I can no longer be patient and ask friendly questions," he went on. "I am now conducting a murder investigation, and no more am I questioning people, I am *interrogating* them. The following people are to report to the lounge. I will interrogate each one individually in the manager's office."

He opened the paper and there was a holding of breaths as he looked over his list, there was a dampness upon brows. Captain Lumumba knew how to sow anxiety.

"George and Harriet Gamble," he read. "Marshall and Sylvia Benedict. Duncan Hawley." He gestured with what he intended as benign dismissal. "The rest of you may go."

And we went!

"What's he going to do to Kenyan tourism?" I complained to Dagger outside. "He's deliberately trying to terrorize us!"

Others were saying, "They're the ones from the van he didn't ride in."

We ran into Richard and Samantha. "Where did that idiot get the idea," Richard said, "that my old man loved Père Javineau liqueur? I'll lay you odds he never heard of it. He couldn't even spell it! That's a name for connoisseurs and if there was one thing my father wasn't, it was a connoisseur. He couldn't tell Scotch from bourbon."

Samantha said, "We all know how terrible your father was. Are you going to buy me a drink or do I have to get one myself?"

"Go do what you want," he snapped at her. "I want to talk to the Gambles; tell them what to do against Lumumba. Those poor people. That monster will eat them alive."

"Which poor Gamble are you worrying about, George or Harriet?"

"You're a fine one to talk. It'll be out the other side of your mouth, when I'm through with you, my beauty."

He went the other way, leaving Samantha with us. "Hah," she said, "that's quite a switch. He used to *hate* George Gamble. Now he wants to save him." Catching herself, she went on brightly, "Perhaps you'll both have a nightcap with me. Do say yes. I hate to drink alone."

It was an invitation I didn't want to accept, but I had to smile and nod. The colonel also nodded; we agreed that would be very nice and went with her into the lounge. A few others were there, Marshall and Sylvia Benedict sitting tight together waiting to be interrogated by the now-fearful captain of police. (Duncan Hawley was already inside, undergoing his session with Lumumba.) At a nearer table, Neville Street was holding Roxanne's hand over a whiskey sour. She gave me a wicked smile, like a saucy little girl to a disapproving uncle. I wanted to thumb my nose at her, but I didn't.

George and Harriet Gamble came in somberly and took seats.

Over our drinks, Samantha tried to explain her problems with Richard. She didn't really think he had a roving eye, she said. They'd never had much of a marriage, but it was his work at the office that left her high and dry. He lived in such deadly fear of his father, he never had time for anything else, including her. That's why she was so into golf. She did tennis, too, and swimming, but golf was her major sport.

"Richard and you don't have much of a life together," I conceded. "No wonder there's so much bitterness between you."

"Oh, now," she answered generously, "you're catching Richard at a difficult time. Usually we get along well. We mind our own business, are polite to each other and keep the wheels oiled. He's not usually such a bastard. Only on this trip."

Colonel Dagger didn't question her, but I couldn't resist. "What's there about this trip that turns him from a Jekyll into a Hyde?"

She gave me a wry smile. "I can't answer that. Perhaps it's being stuck with me twenty-four hours a day instead of an hour or two at cocktails and dinner."

That left me nowhere to go, so I said, "What's going to happen with Richard now?"

"Oh, plenty. He'll be in charge of Cartwright Company. He inherits all his father's stock. He's the new owner and doer. And I suspect he'll try to remove all traces of his father's influence. He'll be a new broom."

"His sudden elevation of George Gamble sounds like a new broom. Is it because his father didn't like George?"

"I think," Samantha mused, "maybe Harriet's caught his eye. I don't know how anybody could like George."

WE HAD TWO DRINKS TOGETHER and broke up. Dagger and I wouldn't let her pay and counted out our Kenya shillings for the waiter just as Marshall Benedict, last of the five to be questioned by Captain Lumumba, came out to rejoin his tense, waiting wife, and we lagged behind as they headed down the path toward the distant bungalows.

When we left the lounge, Neville and Roxanne were still at their cozy, hand-holding table, but Roxanne looked weary. I think Neville wanted to show her his etchings, or maybe only his plastic shower curtain, but she couldn't hide a yawn. That yawn was the best look I'd seen on her face all week.

"Hey," Samantha said when we started along the dimly lit slate path to our distant quarters. She pointed left, into the darkness, toward the wall of large red stones that separated the close-cropped lodge grounds from the high-grown vegetation, the camel path, and marshland that separated us from the distant lake. "See there. Just inside the wall. It's a hippopotamus." She stared again. "And her baby! My God, they really *do* get over the wall."

They were there, all right, barely visible in the blackness of the night, their pinkish hides glistening just enough to enable us to see. And there was nothing but thirty yards of close-cropped grass between them and us on the lighted path. But they stood frozen as statues as we passed on, fifty yards behind the retreating Benedicts, to the distant cabins.

TOMORROW WOULD BE a rest day. Two nights would be spent here, with nothing on tap for Saturday except morning boat rides on the lake for those who were interested, or a trip to a snake farm. It was a time to relax and enjoy. Except for the fact a killer was in our midst.

I dreamed that night of a shadowy murderer chasing Roxanne along that dimly lighted path and woke in a cold sweat at half past three. It was the first nightmare I'd had since I was twelve and I spent the rest of the night, eyes staring into the dim darkness of the ceiling above me, listening to the hippos, their grunts sounding as if they were rooting in the bushes just outside. They sounded so close I finally roused myself in the morning light and went out for a look, but there was nothing to see. They hadn't been up on the lawns and they were gone from the tall grasses, back to the safe waters of the lake.

As for the colonel, I fully expected him to sit outside in the dark all night, downing a liter of Scotch and smoking two packs of cigarettes, but he slept like a baby. I know I don't understand that man.

EIGHTEEN

Saturday, June 28

I WAS YAWNING going to breakfast with Colonel Dagger, but planned only to fill my stomach, return to bed, and sleep the morning away. A ten-o'clock boat ride was the only event on the docket and I knew Neville would have Roxanne preempted for that.

Samantha got into line behind us at the food table where we helped ourselves to pineapple slices, mangoes, grape-fruit, toast, buns, eggs, ham, bacon, sausage, dry cereal, coffee, tea, milk, and the rest of the sumptuous fare these lodges serve their safari guests. I said, "Good morning," and "Where's Richard?"

"I don't know," she answered sourly. "I was going to ask you the same question."

I said I hadn't seen him since he went to tell the Gambles how to deal with Captain Lumumba. "Wasn't he back at the room when you turned in last night?"

"Oh, yes," she answered. "He was there. But he went out—said he wanted to see the hippos, which I don't be-lieve. And he hasn't been back since. Which raises the question of where the hell he slept last night, or with whom."

I noticed that Dagger, ahead of me, hadn't more than nodded a good morning to Samantha and, when he and I had finished serving ourselves, he indicated a table and headed for it without waiting.

She went another way and I breathed a sigh of relief. "I'm
glad we don't have to listen to her at breakfast. Last night
was enough."

"She doesn't seem much concerned about her husband's
peccadilloes," he noted as she set her tray down at a distant
table.

"I thought she seemed a bit distraught."

"It didn't interfere with her appetite, though. That's quite
a trencherman's breakfast she served herself, even for an
athletic woman who has a high metabolic burn rate."

Captain Lumumba entered the room with impact, his
swagger stick, his size, his bright green uniform and polished boots, his gold braid, his dazzle of medals now being
enhanced by his strut. It befit an Oriental potentate roaming the marketplace. He evoked fear among the white tourists. He knew it, he relished it, and it showed.

He pretended to be oblivious. He approached the breakfast table without a glance around and loaded his tray with
such heapings of food as would gag the average diner just
to behold. I suspected that, like his swagger, his medals, and
his sidearms, this was also for show. If he ate like that all the
time, he'd weigh two hundred pounds more than he did.

Aware that all eyes were on him, Captain Lumumba
turned and, as if by accident, brought his laden tray to
where Dagger and I were sitting, placing it on the table next
to Dagger's meal, and taking the chair by Dagger's side.

"You sleeping well?" he addressed the colonel by way of
greeting. "Making any more five-o'clock phone calls?"

It was more of that jousting that went on between them.
He knew who had showed up his botched job and he needed
to get something of his own back in return. "You people
with the white skins love to murder each other, don't you?"
he went on. "Even over here. Perhaps you have no Bibles in

your country? I advise you to read your Bible. There is a message there."

Dagger could take Lumumba's sneers with great composure, but I couldn't help reacting. "You mean the part about Cain slaying Abel?"

"I was thinking," Lumumba answered disdainfully, "of the *New* Testament, the part of the Bible we Christians particularly cherish. Where Jesus says, 'Do unto others.' I believe it's called the Golden Rule."

Dagger took a sip of coffee. "Captain," he said, "I was most interested in your technique last night."

"Technique?"

"Warning the tourists that one of the group is a murderer and that your purpose here was to catch him. It's a technique not generally used in the United States."

"The United States," Lumumba responded haughtily, "does not have a monopoly on wisdom, Colonel."

"True," Dagger replied. "Very true. Which is exactly the reason I asked the question. You obviously have found advantages in this approach which we've been overlooking."

"If you throw a rock into a pond," Lumumba answered, "the fish will scatter. These are the same fish which, a moment before, were behaving placidly, thinking themselves safe. At the splash of the stone, they are startled, and their first instinct is to protect themselves." He raised one quiet black finger, almost as thick as a banana. "The first and primal instinct is to save yourself. I believe Sir Arthur Conan Doyle used this fact as a key point in his story, 'A Scandal in Bohemia.' It was a trick Sherlock Holmes used to get information out of Irene Adler."

Lumumba cast a glance around the room. "Note how all eyes are on us," he said. "But not on you, on *me*. And the whispers are about *me*. Why am I sitting with you? Why not someone else? What do I know? What do I suspect?

"And all the members of your safari tour are worried as to which way my eyes will turn. Even the innocent will hunt inside themselves for guilty motives. They will wonder about their alibis and seek to reinforce them. The one who has no alibi will make every effort to establish one." Captain Lumumba edged closer to Dagger, his face now a scowl. "I want you to know," he said harshly, "that I only talk to you this way because *you* are the one who made the phone call to Nairobi. You have blotched my record." He jabbed that meaty finger against Dagger's shoulder. "And I'm going to make you expunge that blot."

I knew that if one thing drove Dagger to the point of mayhem, it was to be touched and pushed antagonistically. Dagger had his cane and Lumumba had his guns, twin guns in twin holsters, but I would have bet that, in a confrontation, Dagger would have beheaded Lumumba with that deadly cane before the captain could have drawn either pistol.

But nothing happened. Dagger accepted the rough shoving of his shoulder as readily as if it had been done by a crippled passenger on a crowded bus. "Captain," Dagger asked with superior calm, "you threw a stone and you scattered the fish. Has their scattering told you anything?"

"Yes," Lumumba answered with a lift of his chin. "*I* have found the murderer." He looked around with pretended surprise—I say "pretended," for I know enough about police procedure to understand that the police look around *first*. They don't look around *after*.

Lumumba stood up for a better view, milking the terror-effect he had on his audience.

He sat down again, satisfied.

Dagger, who'd played Lumumba's game long enough, grew impatient. "Name him. Who?"

Lumumba wouldn't let go. "Who is missing from your group this morning, Colonel? Even *you* should have spotted it."

"Spotted who's missing? Breakfast doesn't end until nine-thirty. Are you saying anybody who isn't here now has committed a crime?"

The captain was the soul of patience. "I call your attention to Mrs. Richard Cartwright. I believe her first name is Samantha? So where is her husband this lovely morning?"

Dagger said testily, "Come on, Lumumba! If you think Richard Cartwright murdered his father, I hope you've got more to go on than the fact he's not here at breakfast." Dagger jabbed at his eggs and stuffed some into his mouth.

"Hah," Lumumba snorted in return. "You might be interested to know that Mr. Cartwright not only isn't at breakfast, he isn't in this camp. I've had it searched."

"You're saying Richard killed his father?"

Lumumba nodded. "Killed him, realized I was closing in, and fled during the night."

I interrupted. "Why aren't you after him?"

"There's no place he can go," Lumumba answered, "except to his own death." He smiled. "Which saves a trial, saves the government great expense. Very satisfactory solution, wouldn't you say? You people in the States won't kill criminals. You only kill innocent citizens. The criminals you put behind bars, which costs great sums of money. Then, after a little while, you turn them loose and let them kill more innocent citizens. That's because you white people do not know how to kill without guilt. You cannot stand to put a man in an electric chair or gas chamber. You believe you're going against the will of God, against the 'love thine enemy' concept of Jesus Christ.

"There are better ways of handling killers. Right now, your Richard Cartwright is fleeing for his life from nowhere into nowhere. He's afraid I'm going to arrest him, which I would do. And, by escaping the jaws of the lion, he leaps into the jaws of the crocodile. It matters not, so long as the case is solved.''

"But," I said, "how do you know Richard is guilty?"

"We have motive and evidence. And now we have his fear and flight. I threw a rock in the pond and the guilty party gave himself away."

"What's the motive and evidence?" Dagger wanted to know.

Lumumba, sensing challenge, turned a hostile face to the colonel. "That is not your concern," he said. "You doubt his guilt? Perhaps you have someone else in mind?"

Dagger was placating. "He's the logical culprit from what little I know about the case. I'm curious only because I'm an ex-detective."

Lumumba let himself be soothed. "The motive is obvious," he said, his roving eyes keeping everyone else far from our table. "Richard Cartwright murdered his father to inherit his kingdom. It's one of the commonest motives in history. The king bears a son and the son, in time, wants the throne. But the king doesn't want to give it up." He leered a little. "If you know your history, Colonel Dagger, you will know the truth of this statement."

"And the evidence against him?"

"First, there is the fact that Père Javineau liqueur was his father's favorite. Who but the son would know that? Then there is the manager of the Masai Mara Lodge. When the case reopened, I went back and talked to him further. He admitted under my interrogation that he had, in fact, lied when he denied any knowledge of the bottle. He confessed that he had, on the contrary, received a phone call asking him to have a porter deliver the bottle and card, which would be found on the top shelf of the broom closet in the men's lavatory, to Mr. Phineas Cartwright. The manager is prepared to swear that the voice on the telephone belonged to Mr. Cartwright's son, Richard."

Captain Lumumba ingested a huge mouthful of food, washed it down with coffee, and was feeling less hostile. "There is, of course, negative evidence as well," he went on. "Though Phineas Cartwright was not an attractive man, there is no one else with a motive to kill him. More than that, there's not a single shred of evidence to connect anyone else with the case. So, what do we have?" He counted on his meaty fingers. "Richard knew his father's favorite liqueur. That's point òne. Point two: Richard shopped without his wife in Nairobi the day before coming here. That's when he purchased the liqueur. We don't know yet how or when he acquired the poison, but we'll find that out in time. Point three: there's the manager who recognized his voice on the telephone wanting the liqueur picked up from where he'd hidden it, and taken to his father."

I wondered when Dagger was going to puncture Lumumba's balloon by reporting Richard's statement that his father had never heard of Père Javineau liqueur, but Dagger was content only to listen.

Lumumba chewed and swallowed another huge mouthful of food. "Lastly, of course, there is his disappearance. No vans or vehicles are missing, which means he's on foot. But flight from these game parks on foot is hopeless. If he stays on the roads, he'll be arrested. If he stays away from the roads, the animals will get him. One way or another, Richard Cartwright's time has come."

Lumumba had no chance to deal with the matter further, for, at that moment, the young camel boy came bursting into the dining hall.

"Captain, Captain," he cried out, running among the tables to the large man's side. "Out there, out there," he pointed, wild-eyed. "Out by the camel path! There's a dead man!"

NINETEEN

CAPTAIN LUMUMBA strode out with the excited, frightened lad while Dagger and I followed close behind. It was the first dead body the camel boy had ever seen, he told Lumumba. He was bringing the camel along the path for the day's business and he'd seen the body lying in the deep grass close by.

Lumumba, once outside, summoned two of his men, told them all tourists were to remain back of the wall on the lodge grounds. He, meanwhile, followed the lad down to where the camel was tied and back along the beaten path in the direction of our cabins, while the colonel and I, and the other breakfasters, who'd all left their meals upon hearing the news, kept pace along the inside of the stone wall.

From our higher vantage point, we saw the body before Lumumba and the camel boy got to it. It was lying on its back on our side of the camel path, nearly hidden in the dense tall grasses, and had been horribly trampled and mutilated. The skull was broken, half the face smashed, but the clothes and remaining features were recognizable. The dead man was Richard Cartwright.

Dagger, beside me, planted a foot on the wall, leaned forward on his cane, and studied the scene till others began to congregate around us. Then he turned, saw Samantha approaching, and hurried to intercept her. They spoke quietly, a distance away, she with tightened mouth.

Lumumba and the boy were at the body now, the boy overcoming his first fear and shock, gaining interest in the remains. Behind me, someone said, "What happened?" and a voice, almost breaking with emotion, cried out, "The hippos! The damned hippos!"

Spectators crowded closer and Dagger, at Samantha's insistence, led her forward. She came up beside me, took one look, and turned away. "The damned fool," she exclaimed with an air of finality.

Down in the dense grasses, Lumumba was on one knee going through the dead man's pockets, looking over the things he found and putting them back. His conversation with the boy was barely audible and in Swahili, but we watchers could tell by the lad's gestures that he was describing how he'd brought the camel along the path, saw the body, was shocked, then ran for the lodge as fast as the reluctant camel would let himself be pulled.

Harriet Gamble put an arm around Samantha's shoulders, both standing apart with their backs to the wall. George was right up front, one foot on the wall, leaning forward to watch everything Lumumba was doing. Last night, Richard, as new owner of Cartwright, was promising him the world. I wondered what George was thinking now.

Busby Morgan, young and lean, with glasses, mustache, and the inevitable baseball cap, came across the grass with the lodge's manager. One glance at the body turned Busby grayish green and he hurried forward. "Good God," he said to Dagger, "that makes two deaths on one safari. The Bird Watchers Society will be ruined. Didn't anybody tell him don't *ever* get between a hippo and the water?"

Roxanne and Lise Smith approached on their way to breakfast. "Now I don't want to eat," Lise said when she learned what had happened. Roxanne's response was, "Did anybody hear anything?"

I confessed I'd heard the hippos grunting through the late hours of the night. "But nothing that sounded as if they were alarmed or upset."

"When could it have happened? Who saw him last?"

"Samantha. When she got home. But he went out after that, but I don't know what time. How about you? You came in later. Did you happen to see him?"

"We didn't see a soul."

She meant herself and that wretch Neville Street, of course.

Beyond, in the grasses, Captain Lumumba, sweating in his hot, bedecked uniform, but wearing a pleased smile, left the body and approached the wall. "Colonel Dagger," he said, looking up at my tall, lean companion resting on his gold-handled cane, "perhaps you will come with me and confirm the solution of a most unfortunate crime?"

Lumumba meant to nail him for that anonymous phone call, force him to confirm the new solution. The captain and the colonel matched stares, then Colonel Dagger answered, "I would like a witness. Mr. James Addison will accompany me."

"Granted." Lumumba smiled. He could be generous, the game was his. In his mind he was already halfway back to Narok.

We climbed over the wall with an assist by Lumumba's police and tramped through the tall grasses to the corpse. Richard Cartwright was an ugly sight, trampled on, bitten, ribs crushed, skull broken.

"There's your evidence," Lumumba said, indicating the remains. "He panicked and fled. He'd been warned to stay to the paths in the dark. He'd been told not to cut a hippo off from the water. But he forgot everything. He saw the forces of justice closing in. Do you not agree, Colonel?''

Dagger nodded absently, eyeing the body while he listened. Suddenly he bent and pulled up the sleeve of Richard's right arm. "Captain," he said, indicating the bared wrist, "did you happen to notice that Richard Cartwright always wore two wristwatches?''

"Yes, I noticed." The captain stared as if hit by an axe. I looked, too, and suffered the same response. There was no watch.

Lumumba pulled himself together. "Search the area," he thundered to his men. "A watch is missing. Find it!" He rubbed a great hand over his large jaw and, despite himself, his shoulders sagged and his eyes looked sick. "By Jehovah's beard," he moaned. "It's impossible."

Around us, Lumumba's men, four of them, bent and combed the sandy area, but, though the captain, Dagger, and I helped, we instinctively knew that the watch hadn't been lost, it had been taken.

In desperation, Captain Lumumba went to his knees beside the body and forced the sleeve up the forearm until it ripped. The effort was fruitless. There was no wristwatch. Lumumba gave up and got slowly to his feet, where he watched miserably while his men searched ever farther from where we stood.

Dagger said quietly, "I don't think the camel boy took it."

Lumumba shook his head. "No more than the hippos took it."

"It was on his wrist last night when we left the movie."

"It's not in his pockets," Lumumba said dolefully. "Somebody's taken it."

"It doesn't look as if it could be anything but murder then," Dagger said. "His head—" He pointed at the broken skull with his cane. "That looks more likely done with a rock from the stone wall than the foot of a hippopotamus."

Lumumba nodded agreement. "Somebody caught him alone, smashed his head, took the watch, and dumped his body over the wall for the hippos." He straightened his shoulders. "The watch on the right wrist was the better watch," he said, "but it wasn't robbery. His money and rings are intact."

The police captain gave Dagger a wry smile. "I fear my hopes got the better of my wits," he admitted. "The murderer is still among us, but now he has claimed *two* victims. And I must start the hunt anew."

He resumed his air of command. He barked orders to his men in Swahili, pointing at the dead man. He said to Dagger, "We will leave now. My men will wrap the body and take it away. I've got to talk to his wife."

TWENTY

Saturday, June 28

NOBODY, not even the bird watchers, went boat riding on Lake Baringo that morning. The tour group was mesmerized and numbed, and all had to be on hand for interrogation by Captain Lumumba. He set up shop again in the manager's office, with a policeman secretary at his elbow, an armed sentry at the door, and a courier to produce the suspects on demand.

Samantha Cartwright, Richard's widow, was the first to undergo Lumumba's inquisition. It was a fifteen-minute session, at the end of which she was dispatched with the body in one of the vans for Nairobi. They were gone by half past nine, in a cloud of dust.

Singly, one after the other, the rest of us were called before the huge, menacing police captain. After Samantha, he questioned the safari members in the order of their residency in the duplex cabins set in a semicircle at the end of the grounds. Duncan Hawley, who occupied the left half of the duplex nearest the wall, was first on the carpet. Following were Sylvia and Marshall Benedict, who occupied the other half.

Next came Lucy Children and Jennifer Long. They shared their duplex with Samantha, and Richard and Captain Lumumba questioned each, especially Jennifer, at length.

Most of our safari group sat, as I did, in the lounge outside the manager's office, waiting our turn and sweating. I kept notebook and ballpoint in hand to hide my own nervousness.

Not so Lise Smith, however, and not so Colonel Dagger. They chose to retire to quarters and wait for a summons. I thought the colonel would be eager to study the behavior of the group but, as usual, I guessed wrong.

Neville Street was beside Roxanne as usual. He had her crowded against the arm of one of the lounge couches, but Roxanne, for once, wasn't paying attention to him. All she could do was watch the office door through which the suspects—for that's what we were—came and went.

After Jennifer Long had had her turn with Lumumba, Harriet and George Gamble were called. They were in the next bungalow, just a few yards away from Samantha and Richard.

Peter Tower followed them, for he and Neville shared the other half of the Gamble bungalow. He was in with Lumumba a good ten minutes, longer than anyone except Jennifer Long, who had been questioned for fifteen. (I was recording times in my notebook. This would be one helluva travel article when I got through!)

When he finally reappeared, white-faced but, I thought, relieved, it was Neville Street's turn. Neville rose, staring trancelike at the ominous door, then realized with a start that Peter was waiting to preempt his seat beside Roxanne. The thought of abandoning his lady love to the wiles of another, equally predatory, male caused a stricken look to cross Neville's face. He didn't know how much of a lady love he'd have left when he returned.

Neville was back in six minutes, but he had to find a new place to sit, and Peter looked triumphant.

Peter didn't enjoy his advantage long, however. Roxanne and Lise shared the left half of the next duplex, and Rox-

anne was next summoned into Lumumba's presence while
the courier fetched Lise.

Dagger and I had the other half of that bungalow and
Dagger came in with her. It had turned into one of his bad
days, and he arrived relying heavily on his cane, hiding pain.
Without a glance at me, he took what seat was available, a
single against the wall.

Roxanne emerged from a prolonged encounter, white and
uneasy and, seeing her father, went directly to his side,
standing against him with a hand on his shoulder. Though
he sat stolidly, giving no sign, some inner sensitivity told her
he ached and she stayed by him, though he ignored her
solace.

Lise Smith was in and out in no time. After twenty-five
years, she was a Kenyan, not a tourist, an ally, not a suspect.

I was called next and entered the small office trying to do
what good detectives should always do: appraise my surroundings. It didn't work. All that registered on me was the
formidable figure of Captain Lumumba, the brilliant gold
of his epaulets, braid, and medallions contrasting vividly
with the ominous blackness of his skin and his soul-
searching eyes.

He was leaning toward me, his arms on the desk. "Mr.
Addison," he said, in tones as alien as if he were from Mars,
"when and where did you last see Richard Cartwright
alive?"

It sent a shiver of guilt through me, though I didn't know
why, and I hesitated a moment to make sure of my facts before responding. "It was right after the movie last night,
right after you told us—"

"I know what I told you. Get to the point. How was he
acting? Scared? Nervous?"

"He was angry."

"At what?"

"That you were going to interrogate the Gambles."

"Why should that make him angry?"

"He thought you'd frighten and upset them."

"Why should that matter to him?"

"I don't really know, except he seemed to be favoring them."

"What did he think *he* was going to do about it?"

"He went to talk to them, tell them how to handle you."

Lumumba snorted at the thought. "Whom else did you see?"

"His wife was with him. When he left, she, Colonel Dagger, and I had a couple of drinks together in the lounge."

"Who else was there?"

Except for Roxanne and Neville, I had trouble remembering. "Roxanne Dagger, Neville Street. And there were the people you were interrogating."

It went on like that, he directing my answers with short, sharp questions. When had Samantha, Dagger, and I left the cocktail lounge? Whom had we seen on the paths? What time was it?

I explained that we'd left right after he had finished interrogating Marshall Benedict and we'd walked back to the cabins about twenty yards behind them.

"Did you see Richard Cartwright during this time?"

"No, sir."

"Did you see Mr. and Mrs. Benedict go into their cabin?"

"Yes. Well, maybe I didn't actually see them enter, but where the path divides, they took the one to their cabin."

"What did you, the colonel, and Mrs. Cartwright do?"

"We parted where the path branches. She took the one to her cabin, the colonel and I went to ours."

"Did you see her enter her cabin?"

"I glanced that way as the colonel and I were entering ours. She was going in."

"Was there anyone inside when she entered?"

"I don't know. I was two cottages away. I didn't *see* anybody, if that's what you mean."

"That's what I mean. How about lights? Was she going into a dark cabin or a lighted one?"

"I don't remember. But I think it was lighted."

"Do you think Richard was inside, waiting for her?"

"I don't know whether anyone was there or not. But I would assume he was there and waiting since I hadn't seen him anywhere else."

"You *assume* Richard was there in the cabin, waiting for his wife, but the last time you saw him, he was going the other way, off to talk to Mr. and Mrs. Gamble."

"Yes, but that was a long time before—before you talked to the Gambles, before Samantha and the colonel and I had our two drinks."

"You and the colonel then did what?"

"We went to bed."

"And to sleep?"

"To sleep, yes, but not for long." I told of waking at three-thirty and not having been to sleep since.

"What did you hear during those hours you lay awake? Any cries or strange sounds?"

I had to confess I hadn't heard anything but the hippos grunting.

"Before you went to sleep, what did you hear?"

"Nothing."

"No sounds of a quarrel, of people fighting?"

"No, sir."

"You say you woke at three-thirty. How do you know what the time was? Did you look at a clock?"

"I looked at my watch."

Lumumba made a note on his pad. "You may go." He looked beyond me to his sentry. "Colonel Dagger next," he said.

TWENTY-ONE

Saturday, June 28

CAPTAIN LUMUMBA didn't complete his interrogation of the safari group until lunchtime, during which period all of us, with the exception of Colonel Dagger, sat immobile in the lounge watching each other go in and come out of his office with the mesmerization of TV addicts viewing a daytime soap.

Colonel Dagger, as always, was the exception. He limped off after his session with Lumumba and wandered around the grounds in solitude. His leg was hurting and I didn't know whether he was working out the pain or was lost in thought. His departure left Roxanne unattended, of course, and, for the record, in the race that followed, Peter beat Neville to her side for a change.

The colonel was back for the lunch break and Roxanne, to my surprise, shook Peter long enough to join us. I thought it was because of Dagger's pain, but she wanted to talk about the case. "This is all such a mess," she moaned. "I don't know how such things can happen."

Dagger, who'd been withdrawn ever since the discovery of Richard's body, was still preoccupied and disinclined to talk.

"What," I asked Roxanne, "did Captain Lumumba ask you?" I hoped Dagger would come out of his woolgathering if Roxanne could produce new information.

"Oh," she said, "he wanted to know everything I'd done since the movie ended last night—whom I was with, whom

I spoke to, what was said. Especially, what did Neville and I talk about! I told him that was none of his business. He told me it *was* his business and we had a bit of a go-around about that. For a minute or two, I thought he was going to arrest me on grounds I'd met Richard late at night, hit him on the head with a rock, and pitched him over the wall, but even *he* recognized the futility of such a charge."

"Why didn't you tell him what you and Neville talked about? Was it that much of a secret?"

She shook her head. "No, it wasn't that much of a secret, but it was personal. And I don't talk about my personal matters to strangers. Not even to friends. So why should I tell them to an officious policeman who thinks he can bully me?"

"He might have given up the idea that you killed Richard, but what about Neville? Did that give Lumumba ideas about him?"

"Oh, good heavens. Neville?" She sniffed. "What on earth would he want to kill Richard for? Besides, when we went to our quarters nobody else was around. I think we were the last ones to turn in. Lise was dead to the world, your lights were out. I don't think there was a light in any of the other cabins."

"What time was that?"

Roxanne frowned. "I don't know. When did they close the bar? Probably around half past twelve."

I wished Dagger would probe her tête-à-tête with Neville. I suspected the talk was of love and romance, with broad hints by Neville that this was not just two ships passing in the night, that there would be more to come once we all returned to the States. I was intensely curious about that, and intensely jealous.

Unfortunately, Dagger, who'd watched over her like a suspicious husband throughout the first part of the trip, seemed now to have lost interest. I don't know if he thought she was in a safe harbor in Neville's arms, due for wedlock instead of a fate worse than death, but he was as apathetic about her plight as he was about her presence.

Busby Morgan stopped by our table. "I've just been talking with the captain," he said. "He's not going to make any arrests yet, but he's not going to hold us here, either. We're all going on to Camp Samburu tomorrow morning as scheduled. Baringo doesn't have room. A new safari group is coming in tomorrow."

"What about the investigation?" I asked.

Busby said, "That will proceed. Captain Lumumba will travel with us until he finds the person who did these things."

"Is he getting close?" Roxanne wanted to know.

Busby shrugged. "He hasn't told me anything, but he's just been on the phone to Narok. I was in the outer office, and while I don't know the language, I think he was getting chewed out. He had to report a second murder, and it took place while he was on the scene. I think he's in trouble with the authorities. When he was talking to me after, he looked pale and shaken—if anybody with skin his color can look pale.

"We leave tomorrow as planned," he said in parting. "Don't forget, it's a long, six-hour trip. The breakfast hall will open at six-thirty and we want to leave at half past seven."

He went on to the next table and a concerned Roxanne leaned toward her father. "Papa, you're a detective. Do you know who did it?"

Dagger, seeming to note her for the first time, shook his head. "No, I don't know."

"Don't you have any ideas?"

"I don't know enough about the case. I don't know who's alibied. I don't know what evidence Lumumba's got. I'm in the dark about the whole thing."

"You're not totally in the dark, Papa. You do know *some* things."

Dagger gave his daughter a slight smile. "I know Phineas died from drinking from a bottle of poisoned Père Javineau liqueur, which was either brought in from the States or purchased in Nairobi, and that he was carrying a note from Harriet Gamble in his pocket. I know that Richard was hit on the head with a rock, robbed of the watch on his right wrist, and thrown over the wall for the hippos." He shook his head. "That's not a lot to go on."

I broke in. "You say it was Harriet Gamble who wrote the note that she had to see him?"

"Yes, but that hardly makes her a murderess."

"The liqueur was Phineas's favorite," Roxanne reminded him. "That should be important."

"What's really important is that it wasn't Phineas's favorite—if Richard was telling the truth. And that's a rare and expensive liqueur, so it's a question why was that particular brand purchased? Was it to impress him? Was it—?" He stopped, shook his head, and took another mouthful of omelet. "That's enough," he said. "The wise man doesn't speculate when he's got nothing to speculate with."

"Captain Lumumba's in trouble," Roxanne reminded him. "You heard what Busby said. If you offered to help him, he might tell you everything he knows. Then you wouldn't have to speculate anymore."

Dagger shook his head at his daughter's innocence. "Captain Lumumba," he said, "is a very proud man. He's also a bigot. The next to last thing he would do would be to ask for help. The *last* thing he'd do would be to ask help from a white man."

"I think men are stupid creatures," Roxanne said in vexation. "How can somebody like that Captain Lumumba let pride stand in the way of solving the case? If he can't solve it, it could be the end of his career! Kenya can't let tourists come in here and be murdered."

"I'm sure," Dagger answered, "that if the government feels he needs help, they'll assign him help, whether he asks for it or not."

"But you could help him, if he'd let you."

"Maybe I could. I don't know."

"Couldn't you solve it if you were on this case? According to everything I've heard, you were a wonderful detective."

"If you say so."

"And if you helped him solve it, then the authorities would think he did it himself and wouldn't have to assign other people to him, and his career would be saved."

Dagger said to me, "My daughter has a heart as big as the U.S. debt."

"Papa," she said, putting both hands on his sleeve, "you've got to offer your services to Captain Lumumba. You've got to get him out of this!"

"Now stop that," Dagger said. "I'm not going to insult Captain Lumumba by suggesting I can solve his cases better than he can. And I'm not going to leave myself open for the kind of rebuff I'd get. Do you take me for a fool?"

"Oh, you men," she said in vexation. "Yes, I do! You and your arrogant pride. Pride, with you men, goes before *everything*—not just before a fall. I wonder how many wars could have been prevented if it weren't for male pride." She put her hands on her hips. "Here we have a murderer in our midst. Somebody right here, in this room probably, eating at one of these tables. And who knows whom he'll kill next?" She put a finger to her chest. "It might be me! But you men don't care. Solving the case isn't as important as salving your pride. Papa," she said, picking up her fork again, "I think you're just as disgraceful as Captain Lumumba."

I thought, now that she'd had her say, that was the end of it. I should have known better. As we left the dining room, Roxanne seized her father's arm and pulled him toward the manager's office and the solemn, khaki-clad, armed policeman on guard. "I've got to see Captain Lumumba right away," she told the sentry. "Tell him it's very important."

The policeman opened the door and spoke Swahili through the gap while Dagger, squirming in Roxanne's grip, complained, "Now stop it. What are you trying to do?"

The next moment, a grim and foreboding Captain Lumumba loomed in the entrance, his resplendent uniform, with its gleam and green, the medals, the gold braid, and the omnipresent white birch swagger stick, with its leather handle and wrist strap, providing him with all the trappings of power any position could require.

If he'd been taken to task by his superiors, it didn't show. If he were in distress about the case, it didn't show. All that came through was an innate hostility and a resentment that not just a white person, but a *female* white person should intrude upon his affairs.

"Yes?" He fixed his gaze on Roxanne, not deigning to notice either Colonel Dagger or me.

Roxanne seized Lumumba's arm. "Captain," she said, trying to draw him forward, "I want you to meet Colonel Dagger. Colonel, this is the captain. There is a mystery to be solved. Who killed Phineas and Richard Cartwright? Both of you want to know. You can help each other to a solution."

Both Dagger and Lumumba looked awkward. If either had known what purpose Roxanne had had in her pretty

little head, both would have been in flight in opposite
directions. As it was, Lumumba shot Dagger a quick, suspicious look, and said to Roxanne, "I do not need help.
What do you think you're doing?"

"But you *do* need help," Roxanne protested. "For in-
stance, did you know that Père Javineau liqueur was *not*
Phineas Cartwright's favorite liqueur at all?"

Lumumba scowled at her, then at Dagger. "What are you
saying?" he demanded, and jerked his thumb at the colonel. "He tell you this?"

"That's right. And you didn't know it, did you?"

Lumumba ignored her. He turned on Dagger. "*You dared*
tell me otherwise?"

Dagger, facing Lumumba's rage, gently tapped his cane
on the tiles between his feet. "I have told you *nothing*," he
said in his very quiet voice, his eyes on his cane, and I sensed
it took him great self-control to keep from committing
mayhem. But Dagger seemed to have that kind of control—like drinking a liter of Scotch and maintaining enough
discipline to make a vital phone call.

Lumumba sensed the explosive force within the colonel
too, and while he didn't exactly back off, he eased matters
a little. "You have such information?"

Dagger stilled his tapping cane. "Only on Richard Cartwright's say-so."

Lumumba scowled. This put a new light upon things for
which he was not ready. "Why didn't you tell me this before?"

"You mean during your interrogation?"

Since that was the only time he could have produced the
information, from the silence that fell between them, I knew
that, as with me, Lumumba had given Dagger no chance to
do more than give strict answers to strictly phrased questions.

"And," Roxanne went on, interrupting the painful silence, "did you know, Captain Lumumba, that the note found in Phineas Cartwright's jacket pocket, the one that said, 'I must see you at once, it's important,' was written by Harriet Gamble?"

Lumumba turned again on Colonel Dagger. "You say that?"

Dagger nodded. "That's right."

"How do you know?"

"I took handwriting samples among the women and matched them."

"You took *handwriting* samples?" Lumumba's surprise descended to new rage. "What did you do that for? Did someone give you to think you were working on this case?"

Now Dagger, in the face of Lumumba's new indignation, changed his own manner. "Nothing like that, Captain," he said respectfully. "Consider me, instead, like an old firehorse, long retired from action, but still leaping up and snorting to go when the alarm bell sounds."

Lumumba stared at him. "What're you saying? You're a horse? What's a fire-horse?"

"A figure of speech, Captain. An American figure of speech. Long outmoded. Long forgotten. Blame it on my age. I'm trying to say that a lifetime in given areas forms given habits, and even if the time has passed, the habits remain. I'm a victim of habit, Captain." Then he changed subjects. "As for the note, I'm sure you're not being told something you don't already know when my daughter says Harriet Gamble wrote it."

"This I know," Lumumba answered sonorously. "Such discoveries are not beyond the reach of the Kenyan police."

"This I well know," Dagger answered. "Which is why I told my daughter not to bother you." He heaved a sigh.

"Perhaps in Kenya, it is different, but in America, daughters seem to develop a mind of their own."

"A pity," Lumumba said. "In Kenya, it is better."

"I hope you're satisfied," Dagger said to Roxanne when we got free and headed out of the lodge. "What I recommend for you is a long afternoon of minding your own business."

"Sorry about that, Papa," Roxanne answered. "I only wanted to help." She turned and waved at a loitering Peter Tower. "There's Peter. He's asked me to go on the tour of the snake farm with him."

Dagger humphed in obvious displeasure and limped on. I was displeased, too, and lingered with her long enough to say, with a certain surliness in my tone, "For someone who started out eager to take care of her father, you seem to have developed quite a casual attitude toward his well-being."

"Oh," she answered, giving my sleeve a friendly pat, "I know he's perfectly safe in *your* hands. And he *likes* you, too!"

She turned and was gone.

TWENTY-TWO

Sunday, June 29

THE SAFARI GROUP hit the road at twenty minutes of eight that Sunday morning. Six hours of driving to Camp Samburu, scheduled to arrive in time for a late lunch. Not much game viewing with so far to go, but the group wasn't in the mood anyway. Richard's murder had laid a pall over the whole safari and a cloak of fear over the Cartwright contingent. Would the villain strike again? Who next? Surely the killer had to be mad! But that was the most frightening thing of all: no one in the group appeared the least bit unhinged.

We were short one van. Amram Kitanyi had transported Samantha, accompanying Richard's remains, back to Nairobi, so Roxanne, Dagger, and I were split up among the vans that remained. I was cast in with the bird watchers, meaning the Baldwins, the Kirbys, and old Sidney Leggett, who didn't let murder interfere with his hobbies and who proudly told me he'd added forty new birds to his life-list. The Kirbys and Baldwins fought the impact of the two deaths by helping him see more: "There! On that twig! Four trees to the left of—" "On that bush, close to the ground!"

Dagger rode with Duncan Hawley, the Benedicts, and the Gambles. At least he was with people who counted. With Richard dead, Marshall was now the man in the company to be reckoned with. Gamble, who'd been elevated by Richard, must now be buttering up Marshall. And Harriet was the one who'd written the urgent note found in

Phineas's pocket. All kinds of interesting things would be going on in *that* van. Lucky Dagger.

Guess where Roxanne was—in with Peter Tower and Neville Street! It didn't matter which one of them had rigged it, that arrangement had been *rigged*!

Of course, if I'd been on the ball, I could have done a little rigging on my own. But she'd have known I'd done it and I've made it a rule never to join the pack and all of us run after the same girl. The girl in question will never be able to tell *you* apart from the others. As I stated in my "Manhattan as a Bachelor's Paradise" article, being *memorable* was the key to success.

Right then, though, I was doubting my theory. Peter and Neville were unabashedly trying to outrun each other in their pursuit of Roxanne, and she knew who they were, all right. As for me, who played it laid back and cool, all she saw in me was a caretaker for her father.

Of course, Roxanne wasn't *alone* with Peter and Neville. Lucy Children and Jennifer Long rode in that van, too. Until now, they'd been having those two handsome eligible bachelors to themselves, and I could imagine they'd find Roxanne's new membership in the company as welcome as a visit from a sister's quintuplets.

There were three other riders on the trip. Busby Morgan was in with Roxanne; Lise Smith rode with Dagger; and Captain Lumumba—what else?—was in with the bird watchers and me. He'd have got more clues from the Cartwright bigwigs, but that's where *Dagger* was riding, and I could guess Lumumba was damned if he'd anymore be caught riding in the same van as the colonel. And I guess, after his encounter with Roxanne, he was damned if he'd ride with the colonel's daughter, either. That left him with me.

I was also left with six hours of riding over rough roads with nobody I wanted to talk to and nobody who wanted to talk to me. Their minds were on birds, mine was on murder. I hunched down in my seat and thought about it.

There were now ten members of the Cartwright contingent, and one of them had murdered two people. (A murderer for each was out of the question.) That meant the villain was one of ten people: Marshall and Sylvia Benedict, Samantha Cartwright, Lucy Children, George and Harriet Gamble, Duncan Hawley, Jennifer Long, Neville Street, and Peter Tower.

What evidence did we have? The manager of the Masai Mara Lodge swore it was Richard who phoned to have the liqueur delivered to his father. His identification had been wrong, but unquestionably the voice had been a man's. That eliminated the Cartwright women (Sylvia, Samantha, Lucy and Jennifer), reducing the number of suspects to five: Marshall Benedict, George Gamble, Duncan Hawley, Neville Street, and Peter Tower.

The next question was: who could have killed Richard? Armed with a rock, obviously anyone could.

How about dumping him over the wall into the hippos' den? That was a different matter. Marshall Benedict? He was a huge man, the wall was only two feet high, and the body didn't need to be more than rolled over it. He could have done it in his sleep.

George Gamble? He was more than virile enough.

Duncan Hawley? I'd rule out Duncan. I doubted he could drag Richard's body across the ground, let alone get it over a wall.

Neville Street and Peter Tower? They were the youngest and strongest of the lot. They were the ones most able, single-handedly, to dispose of Richard.

That reduced me to four suspects. What else was there?

Who would profit from such deaths? In alphabetical order: Marshall Benedict had been third in command. Now he
was in the catbird seat. George Gamble profited by Phineas's death, but suffered from Richard's. Hawley had been
eliminated. Neville and Peter? They were in sales. Unless
personal animosities were involved, they were motiveless.

That left only Marshall Benedict. But what about Duncan Hawley? Never mind that he "couldn't have done it,"
did he have motive? He roomed with Phineas on Phineas's
orders, and there were rumors he knew where the skeletons
were buried. If that were true, I'd expect him to be the victim, not the murderer.

So much for motive. What could I deduce for opportunity?

Anybody could have phoned the manager at the Masai
Mara and sent the poisoned liqueur to Phineas. As for
Richard, Samantha said he went out after she returned and
never came back. At the time she returned, escorted by
Dagger and me, the only safari people still in the cocktail
lounge were Roxanne and Neville. Everyone else had supposedly retired. Of course, maybe some of them had *not*
retired. We'd need to check all alibis thoroughly.

I nodded in satisfaction. That was where the gleam of
light should occur. Richard wasn't going out to see the hippos. Ridiculous thought. He was going to meet someone.
And he didn't know that the someone was going to kill him
and take the watch off his right wrist. (We mustn't forget
that missing watch. That's got to be a most important clue.)
And then that someone would throw his body over the wall
for the hippos to abuse.

But whom would Richard want to meet? What could it be
about at such an hour? Why secret and in the dark? Why
was the watch involved?

I sighed in bewilderment. So many questions I couldn't begin to answer. But if I couldn't provide answers, neither could Lumumba. He rode up front with the driver, but hardly spoke. He was, instead, bent over an open notebook scribbling in additions. And Captain Lumumba would have already checked all alibis. If that gleam of light really existed, *he'd* have found it.

WE HAD AN UNSCHEDULED pit stop at ten minutes of ten, out in the middle of nowhere, in vast, sparse, flat land, miles between villages. Roxanne's van had developed a soft front tire and van no. 4, Dagger's, was having engine trouble.

Roxanne's driver changed tires in a breeze while the other two drivers removed the seat of van no. 4 to get at the engine and remove the distributor. As for us safari tourists, we wandered around the nearby fields, some taking the opportunity of relieving themselves behind bushes, the bird watchers scanning the plains with binoculars for sightings, the Cartwright people talking and mingling warily. They weren't afraid of the animals, they were afraid of each other!

It gave me pause. I'd been brought up thinking of Africa as dangerous country, so filled with savage beasts that your life was at risk the moment you set foot beyond the bounds of civilization. But the only killers in Africa, outside of man, are the carnivores and they stay close to the herds that feed them. In all the vast, sparse plain around us here, no creature was to be seen except an occasional bird.

Lumumba spent the pit stop aboard our van. I chose to stretch my legs and mingle, going to join the Benedicts. My real interest was Roxanne's van, but I wasn't going to let that show. That group had no room for me anyway. Jennifer had Peter off to herself, getting him to do something to her camera, which left Neville with Roxanne and Lucy. Peter was obeying Jennifer's behest, but he didn't like it and his jealous eye was on Neville, who was trying to pry Roxanne away from Lucy Children—except that a determined Lucy wasn't about to let go. It was as I expected. Lucy and Jennifer were trying to quarantine Roxanne in a fruitless effort to keep Peter and Neville to themselves.

Meanwhile, I was with Marshall and Sylvia for the first time since Richard's murder and I tried further investigation on my own.

Sylvia was the nearer so I approached her first. "That's terrible about Richard's death," I said.

Her eyes fixed on mine and she gripped my arm with more strength than I thought was in her. "What do you think's going to happen?" she whispered with fright in her eyes. "Is Marshall going to be next?"

"Marshall? Why?"

"Now he's head of the company. Except he isn't. And I don't think he wants to be head anyway. Who do you think's behind all this? I've never liked Duncan Hawley. Marshall would trust him with his life, but I wouldn't trust him around the corner."

I didn't know what to say to that. "What do you mean Marshall isn't the head of the company?"

"He'd have to have board approval. You don't just step into a job like that."

"But nobody has his expertise."

"Directors don't always pick the logical man."

"Richard didn't seem to need board approval to start elevating George Gamble."

"Richard *inherited* the company. Marshall does need board approval. He's only an employee. Anyway, after what's happened, with Phineas and Richard dead, we don't want it. Let somebody else head Cartwright."

"Who?"

"Give it to Duncan Hawley, since he wants it so much. I don't care. Let it be anybody except Marshall!"

Marshall overheard that last. "How unambitious of you, my dear," he said, joining us. "Why should the leadership of Cartwright Company go to somebody else? Do you think anyone else can handle it better?"

She shook her head mutely, and her hand went to his arm. "No, but I'd rather have a live husband than a dead Cartwright president."

"Ridiculous," he chided her, patting the old gnarled fingers which held his arm. "Whatever the motives somebody had for killing Phineas and Richard, they have nothing to do with me. I'm no threat to anybody." To me he went on. "As Sylvia just told you, I'm nothing without board approval. Whatever the killer's grudge, it can't have anything to do with me."

"What kind of a *grudge* do you think it might be?" I asked. "You've been with the company since its inception. You know more about the inside fighting, the hates and loves of the employees, what Phineas and Richard did to you all. Who do you think's behind these murders?"

Marshall rubbed his chin and looked into the distance. "That's exactly the question Captain Lumumba asked me. Like you, he seemed to think I had an inside track, that I would *have* to know what person in our company—what person on this tour—had the means and motive and boldness to kill old Phineas and his son."

Marshall pointed around at the Cartwrightians. "Look at them," he said. "George and Harriet. George is simpleminded and Harriet has the brains. What of it? Duncan Hawley? He drinks too much, and if I were in his shoes, I probably would, too. But wouldn't you call drinking an antidote to murder? If you drink to forget, you don't have to kill."

Marshall looked further. "Neville Street and Peter Tower," he continued. "Playboys of the western world—except when it comes time to make their mark. They chase girls. Right now, the beauteous Roxanne is their target, the fly on the leaf, waiting to be gobbled up by the chameleon's tongue. Poor thing. She doesn't realize she's the latest trophy to be won. They tied as Cartwright salesman of the year. That's why they're both on the same safari. But they're not satisfied to tie. Both want to be 'first,' and now they've set themselves a *new* goal. Who can woo and win the beautiful Roxanne?"

Marshall's description gave me the chills. This was exactly what I thought they were up to, but I didn't know how to warn Roxanne.

"Then," Marshall went on, "there's Jennifer Long, the company bookkeeper. She's plain and nondescript, the shy, withdrawn type, destined for old-maidhood. Has she told you of her one breakout attempt, how she once went to a singles bar to get picked up and nobody looked at her? It's her favorite story. She tells it on herself with a laugh, like, after that, she was resigned. But look now. She's dragged Peter away to herself—the most aggressive move I've seen her make, probably the second most aggressive move she's *ever* made. But school's out right now. We're on vacation and can kick over the traces. She's got Peter fixing her camera, or showing her how it works. And I'll lay you odds she knows more about cameras than he does. But she sees this as her one chance to escape her fate. She hopes Peter, in the process of adjusting her camera, will glance into her eyes and see, beyond those bifocal lenses, the enthralling depths she's been waiting to have recognized.

"And Lucy. She *knows* three's a crowd, but she thinks maybe she can make Roxanne go away and leave Neville to her. She doesn't stand a chance." He gestured her dismissal. "Lucy was married once and ought to know better.

"So there's the lot. If you can see any one of them murdering old Phineas and Richard, you've got better eyesight than I have."

I didn't have better eyesight. I couldn't see anyone killing anyone. I couldn't believe anyone had—except there were two dead bodies and the only people on hand for both deaths were in view before us.

I gave up the puzzle and joined Dagger. He seemed to have given up on the puzzle, too, for he was watching the drivers at work on the no. 4 van engine. One of them was cleaning a distributor point with a borrowed nail file. "You don't only know birds," I noted. "You know car engines."

He'd worked in a garage, he told me, before he took the safari guide training course. "If we didn't know how to fix cars," he reminded me, "you wouldn't be very safe going where we have to go."

The nail file did the job, the engine started purring, and we were under way once more within half an hour.

TWENTY-THREE

Sunday, June 29

THE DRIVE wasn't too long and arduous after all. We entered Samburu Park at one o'clock and, fifteen kilometers later, disembarked at Camp Samburu at one-thirty.

Lake Baringo was noted for its hippopotami. Samburu, which was a river, was noted for crocodiles. The patio of the main lodge, rimmed by a three-foot stone wall, overlooked the muddy, shallow river in which an occasional crocodile could be seen. Paths through the woods, paralleling the embankment, led to tourist cabins a hundred yards distant.

Even before we'd been assigned quarters, word was out that a nightly ritualistic feeding of the crocodiles took place on the dirt area beside the patio wall. Here they would eat close at hand, as big as life!

Lunch was held in a spacious dining room with large glass panes revealing the outside foliage. The space above was open, and birds darted under the eaves and flew through the room over our heads. Along the top beams, a genet shepherded two babies around posts and along its varnished surface. The genet was a catlike creature, but far more sinuous and supple, moving around posts like a snake.

Roxanne, the colonel, and I chose a table together almost under the wandering genet, and who should come out of nowhere and take the fourth seat but Samantha Cartwright. I don't know if Dagger was as startled as I, but we came to our feet in welcome and I couldn't help saying, "What are you doing here?"

"Amram brought me back after I took care of things in Nairobi. He had to rejoin the group."

"But I thought you'd be going back to the States."

"Oh, come," she answered. "You don't really expect me to go into mourning, do you? How hypocritical do you think I am?"

I fumbled. "I guess I just assumed you'd go home with the body."

"The way Richard went home with his father's? That would have been a dismal trip! Things will get dismal soon enough. I decided to make the most of things here and postpone the future as long as I can."

A FOUR-O'CLOCK GAME DRIVE, so poorly attended that only two vans were needed, was the only thing scheduled for the afternoon. Except for the bird watchers, most of the group stayed home and I should have, too. Game drives were getting to me. The thousandth and first Thompson's gazelle or impala or topi you see is doubtless just as wonderful as the first, but they don't strike you that way. Besides, Dagger and Roxanne didn't come and that took all the fun out of it.

We got back at six-thirty and darkness was falling by the time I reached the patio and the Crocodile Bar where cocktails were served. On the flat dirt surface beyond the wall, a heap of animal entrails had been piled, gray and white under the floodlamps, ready for the crocodiles.

I had a couple of Bloody Marys and waited with the rest of the tourists for the crocs to climb their well-worn trail up from the river for their nightly meal. Humans don't have the patience of other animals and a great many drinks were sold at the Crocodile Bar before, ultimately, appearing over the brow of the embankment, two crocodiles made their way, the first large, the second huge.

With their inhuman patience, they took enormous time approaching the food, all the while the tourists crowded against the wall for a prime view and it was tough getting a ringside position. Roxanne, as usual, had abandoned her father and me in favor of the Cartwright "twins," as I called Neville and Peter, and Neville was the one who'd copped her this time. He had her so firmly planted against the wall, his body against her body, no more than fifteen feet from the crocs, she must have been getting stone dents in her thighs and—I hoped—holes in her skirt and runs in her panty hose. I wondered if he'd dated her up while Jennifer Long was conning Peter into fixing her camera. If he had, I doubted Peter would speak to Jennifer again.

What interested me about this event was: two terrible murders were totally forgotten as safari tourists crowded against the wall, as enthralled as if we were privileged to witness a prehistoric scene.

The first crocodile at last approached the feast and, in two mouthfuls, gulped such a quantity of entrails that his stomach sagged, and it was only with difficulty that he could pull himself off among the trees, his stomach dragging on the ground, to let his meal digest.

The second and larger of the two then edged in on the remaining heap and gulped down three huge jawfuls. He still couldn't finish off all that was there, but he had so engorged himself that he couldn't move from the spot for half an hour, and then only with difficulty.

Watching crocodiles digest their food for half an hour is like watching the Empire State Building for half an hour. I had myself a third Bloody Mary and was no longer interested in the front-row spot.

Eventually the attention of the hardiest enthusiasts, even Neville and Roxanne, waned and we all went in to a beef-Wellington dinner.

Nothing was on the docket for tonight. We could drink at the Crocodile Bar, or go to our cabins, or watch the prone crocs digest their dinner, or wait for interminably patient smaller crocs to come finish the remains of the entrails.

Or we could think about murder!

CAPTAIN LUMUMBA was much in evidence this evening, roaming restlessly, watching, pondering, ostracized by the safari group, which soon abandoned the bar because of his presence. Colonel Dagger was a loner, too, brooding, leaning on his cane, withdrawn into his own particular world. He didn't want me around, he didn't seem to care where Roxanne had gone. The one thing I noticed was that his and Lumumba's paths did not cross.

By half past nine, the Crocodile Bar was nearly empty. Lumumba still loitered, like a disease, and Colonel Dagger lingered, out on the patio, leaning on his cane, alone at the wall, the only one staring at the immobile crocodiles on the ground beyond.

I told him good night, but he only nodded. He'd be along later, he said, and I wended my way alone back along the path to our cabin.

TWENTY-FOUR

Monday, June 30

"WHERE'S JENNIFER?"

That was the cry at breakfast at Camp Samburu. Jennifer didn't come to eat with Lucy Children and a distraught Lucy said Jennifer's bed had not been slept in. While porters brought our luggage to the vans in preparation for our trip to fabled Crestview Lodge, overlooking an animal watering hole, our final and finest stop, the only concern on the breakfasters' minds was, "Where's Jennifer?"

Captain Lumumba was quickly at the large, hapless Lucy Children's side. Lucy was great as a personal secretary but, in this milieu, she was as helpless as a toddler. She didn't know what had happened to Jennifer, she declaimed in tones all in the dining room could hear. She, Lucy, was an early-to-bedder. Jennifer was in the cabin with her when Lucy retired and that's all she knew. The time? She gauged it as before ten o'clock.

What about Jennifer?

She was in the slow process of getting ready for bed. Jennifer was always slow about things.

"How long does it take you to go to sleep?" That was an alarmed Captain Lumumba, not just asking but demanding.

"I don't know," Lucy whined. "Two minutes? Three minutes? I don't know how to time it."

Lumumba turned elsewhere. "I want this camp searched," he roared at the manager and porters. "These tourists don't leave here until we find that woman!" He pointed at the drivers gathered in the doorway. "You hear that? No one goes anywhere until we find out what happened to this woman!" He pointed to the staff again. "Search every cabin. Search the woods. Search off the paths. She might have gotten lost somewhere."

He turned his attention back to the tourists. "You Americans will remain here in the lodge. You are to go nowhere. No one is to leave. You will line up and I will speak to you singly, after which you will remain in the Crocodile Bar until further notice."

He took a chair at a corner table, got out his notebook, and the rest of us formed a line and one by one advanced to stand at his side and answer questions. Interestingly enough, he summoned Colonel Dagger first and leaned close with his questions, scowling and making notes. But he didn't seem to hate the colonel as much as before, didn't seem quite as suspicious of the detective with the white skin.

Once Dagger was gone, Captain Lumumba took on the rest of us according to place in line. Samantha was ahead of me and the captain took more time with her than the customary thirty seconds. With her, it was more like a minute. When it was my turn, he was as brief as he'd been with the others. He demanded my whereabouts for the previous evening and who else could vouch for what I said.

For the first time, I felt a gnawing in my own stomach. I'd gone to our cabin alone. While I'd seen no one, no one had seen me. Nor did I have any idea when Dagger came in, for, by then, I was asleep. But who was to say I didn't have a late date with Jennifer and knew more about her fate than I'd admitted?

Captain Lumumba, however, appeared to accept my feeble alibi without interrogation. He dismissed me and beckoned to Roxanne, who was next in line. I tarried near the patio entrance wanting to say soothing things to her when she followed, but I found Samantha at my elbow and Roxanne, when she approached, did not look in need of consolation.

In another minute, Lumumba was finished and pushed us aside to order the staff to greater diligence in the search. Despite his bluster and thunder, he looked as miserable as a month-old baby in a rain-soaked carriage.

Deserted by Roxanne and plagued by Samantha, I looked around the patio for Colonel Dagger. To my surprise, he was out beyond the wall roaming on the dirt patch where the now-vanished crocodiles had fed the night before. The innards had vanished, too, consumed by subsequent crocodiles, and the ground was as bare as when we'd arrived the previous noon.

As for Dagger, he moved with purpose, studying the ground, poking among the nearby bushes with his massive gold-headed cane. He even went over the brow of the embankment down the sloping path the crocodiles had worn for themselves until he half disappeared. I was afraid he might go all the way down to the river's edge, but I held my peace.

Roxanne had spotted him, too, but she was less inhibited. "Papa!" she cried out in alarm. "What're you doing?"

He didn't reply, but went farther down the embankment, then stooped and was lost to sight.

Captain Lumumba was at our elbow. He'd heard Roxanne's cry. "Where is he? What's he doing? What's happening here?"

At that moment, Dagger rose into view and Lumumba's mouth gaped. "What the hell are you *doing*!" he bellowed at the colonel. "Come back here. Get your damned hide back where I say!"

Colonel Dagger limped back across the broad stretch of dirt toward the wall and the captain. He was leaning heavily on his cane with his left hand. His limp was bad this morning.

In his right hand he was holding something, but we couldn't tell what until he passed it over the wall to Lumumba. It was a woman's shoe.

The rest of us were crowded around, and Lucy shrieked, "It's Jennifer's," and started to weep.

Lumumba, turning the shoe over and over in his hand, said to the colonel, "What made you look over there?"

"The last person who was missing was thrown to the hippos. I wondered if this one might have been thrown to the crocodiles."

Lumumba turned to the Camp Samburu manager who'd pushed his way to the captain's elbow. "Fetch everyone back here," he ordered. "I want my men here with rifles. We have to retrieve a body."

"Retrieve?" Lucy Children cried out. "There'll be nothing left. The crocodiles have eaten her!"

IT WAS A GRIM GROUP that gathered on the patio fifteen minutes later. Captain Lumumba's khaki-clad minions, five strong, rifles in hand, were lined up under his eye on the patio, just short of the wall. Those of us on safari were drawn back to give them room, but we were clustered as near as we could get. There was no conversation among us above a murmur, and little of that. All eyes were on the Kenyan police captain and all ears were upon his words. It was half past eight and the sun was creeping above the trees, pushing the shadows on the patio aside.

"You're going to have to wade, and you may have to swim," Captain Lumumba told his command. "And we're going to have to kill a few crocs on the way. They aren't going to let you in without a fight. We may have to wipe out the lot of them, but they've got something we want and we're going in there and get it. And you know what it is.'' With that, he slipped over the stone wall onto the feeding ground. "Follow me."

The five armed policemen went over the wall in his wake, followed him to the crocodile trail to the river, and disappeared down the embankment. The rest of us clustered against the wall, pressing our thighs against its uneven sides. We could hear the captain barking commands, but, as usual when he was out of our ken, the language was Swahili.

What else we heard from the riverbank were thrashing and splashings of water, and a number of rifle shots. Too many.

At last it was quiet down there, but that was the worst part. We on the patio had no idea what was going on, but we knew Jennifer had been found and she was dead.

Lucy Children wept on my shoulder about poor Jennifer and her failed dream of one day getting married—despite Lucy's horror tales of her own wedlock. "She didn't want to die a virgin," Lucy moaned, tears streaking her cheeks, "but better *that* than what I went through!" I wasn't sure for whom her tears were shed.

Finally, at the end of fifteen minutes, Captain Lumumba reappeared, his uniform dusty and nonglistening, his boots muddied, his face sweaty. This was not the polished, arrogant authoritarian who had first imposed himself upon our tour. He looked tired and old and defeated. Even his swagger stick was lost from his belt and he didn't seem to know it.

His men straggled up behind, all of them with trousers soaked to the knees, one man totally drenched, as if he'd been diving.

Lumumba, ignoring everyone else, came directly to the wall, face to face with Colonel Dagger. "She's been murdered," he said, addressing the colonel. "Strangled. The marks are on her throat."

Dagger said, "She hasn't been eaten?"

Lumumba shook his head. "Crocodiles have sensitive stomachs. They don't like tough food. When they catch an animal, they don't eat it, they drown it, then store it in an underwater cache for several days until it rots and gets soft. *Then* they eat it." He gestured in dismay. "That's where we found your friend. We have her out on the bank. We'll have to do an autopsy to find out whether she was drowned by the crocs or whether she was already dead. We think she was dead, but we have to be sure. After we're through, the body will be returned to the United States."

Colonel Dagger, leaning on the wall toward the captain, nodded. He said, "What can I do to help?"

Lumumba lowered his voice so only those of us close to the colonel could catch the words.

"Colonel," he said, "you saw fit to fetch the woman's shoe. You look in places my men would not look. You are white. You know the eccentricities of white men. I am black. I do not know your kind. I know my kind. But I must deal with *your* kind. Perhaps you can give me some guidance. Perhaps you can help me understand your kind?"

He was a proud man, Captain Lumumba, and he did not beg. He only asked, and he would not have been surprised had Colonel Dagger refused. But the colonel only planted his stick between his legs and nodded. "It is an honor to be asked," he answered. "May I see the body?"

The captain nodded. "As you wish." He helped Dagger over the wall on his bad leg and they disappeared down to the river, accompanied by Lumumba's men. They reappeared five minutes later and held a hurried consultation in

the middle of the feeding ground, Lumumba's men loitering nearby. Lumumba and the colonel nodded agreement
and returned to the wall.

The police captain planted both hands on the stone top.
"It has been decided," he proclaimed to our tour group,
"that we embark at once for Crestview Lodge, your final
stop on this safari. The government of Kenya apologizes to
you for any inconvenience you have encountered on this
trip. The government of Kenya also hopes that you will understand that any difficulties you have experienced on your
travels here are not the fault of the government, nor of the
Kenyan people."

TWENTY-FIVE

Monday, June 30

WE LEFT FOR CRESTVIEW LODGE at quarter past nine, an
hour and fifteen minutes behind schedule, and it was a silent, anxious group. Jennifer's slaying hit everyone hard.
She was not just a third death, but a third *murder*, and what
mania for killing lay behind what pair of innocent eyes? The
apparent lack of motive had even the bird watchers worried. In fact, the Kirbys and Lucy Children wanted to
abandon the safari and return at once to Nairobi. Lumumba wouldn't let them. We were all suspects in a murder case and no one would be excused no matter how
innocent he seemed.

So the nervous Kirbys, the Baldwins, and old Sidney
Leggett boarded their customary van and only Sidney, his
binoculars and camera forever around his neck, his map and
notebook in his lap, seemed neither to mourn the dead nor
fear for his own fate.

Lumumba assigned the worried but competent Lise Smith
to ride with them, and he made other passenger adjust-
ments as well. With Phineas and Jennifer dead, van no. 3
only held the distraught Lucy Children, Peter, and Neville.
Lumumba assigned the Gambles to ride with them.

That left Duncan Hawley and the Benedicts in van no. 4.
Sylvia Benedict had become terrified of George Gamble.
She was certain her husband was next on the hit list and
George Gamble would benefit. So Lumumba, showing a
human streak for once, made the change. And, he added to
van no. 4 Samantha Cartwright and Busby Morgan. That

left van no. 1 with only four people aboard, Colonel Dagger, Captain Lumumba, Roxanne, and me. Captain Lumumba could thus spend the trip discussing the case with the colonel with only a pair of nonsuspects, sworn to secrecy, to overhear.

The two of them, Dagger and Lumumba, sat in the middle passenger seat, Roxanne and I taking the front one where we could hang onto their every word.

"First," Colonel Dagger said to Lumumba as our van led the way over the bumpy dirt road out of the camp, "how do you see it, Captain? What do you know of what has happened? I need a briefing."

"It was hard to form theories," the captain answered, his notepad, thick with writing, open on his knee, his eyes lowered, trying to hide the shame he felt at having to display his ignorance.

"You know, of course, the details of the first murder, how the lying manager of the Masai Mara at first denied all knowledge of the liqueur bottle and blamed the porter for poisoning Phineas, then admitted receiving the phone call requesting that the bottle be fetched from its hiding place and delivered to the old man. He was wrong in believing the caller was Richard, but we may at least conclude the caller was a man."

Dagger said solemnly, "With a witness as unreliable as the Masai Mara manager, I don't know that we should conclude anything."

"Hmmm," Lumumba answered, and made a note. "Your point is well taken. His lying has been my bane. First he swore it was the porter who poisoned Phineas, and I could believe him, for the lad was a known liar, he'd been abused by Phineas, and his story of finding the bottle on the shelf of the broom closet in the men's lavatory was the kind of ridiculous alibi that an uneducated youth would propose. And lastly, to my eternal chagrin, it never occurred to me that a member of a tour group would kill a fellow member. To commit murder in a foreign country is to invite unbelievable risks." Lumumba spread his hands at such an outlandish idea. "No. If a man wants to kill another man, he does it on his home territory, so he can maximize his safety."

Lumumba slowly shook his head. "Your phone call showed me I was wrong. White people are capable of the unthinkable. So I made the lying manager confess he ordered the bottle delivered, and now he swore it was Richard who phoned the request. Again I believed him. Who but Richard would profit by the old man's death? Who but Richard would know his father's favorite liqueur? Once again I was led astray."

"You aren't to blame for believing Phineas liked that liqueur," Dagger interjected. "I didn't know what else to say to get the poor porter off the hook and suspicion directed at ourselves."

"Nevertheless," Lumumba went on, "I appeared a fool to my superiors." He spread his hands again. "Perhaps I am, for now there are three murders and I do not understand them. I cannot even believe them. Cyanide in a liqueur bottle, a missing wristwatch, a dead bookkeeper? And all on *safari*? I do not know how white people think. Which is why I turn to you."

"What about the note from Harriet Gamble in Phineas's pocket?" Dagger asked. "Did she explain it?"

"Not more than she could help, but putting together what I got out of her and out of her husband, I get this." He checked his notes. "Harriet wants a divorce. George doesn't want to give it to her. Her main reason is he gives her no room. He's extremely jealous, wants her to account for every minute of her time away from him, accuses her of having affairs with every man she meets though, she maintains, she's never been unfaithful to him. George told her on the way to Masai Mara he'd persuaded Phineas to transfer one of the employees to the West Coast branch because he believed Harriet and he were fooling around together. Harriet claimed this was totally false and unfair to the man, who has a wife and family. She handed Phineas the note when they arrived at the lodge and met with him later. Phineas told her he wasn't transferring the man, that he knew all about George and his jealousy. Phineas neglected to dispose of the note, which was why it was still in his pocket.'' Lumumba turned to Dagger. ''That is what I put together from the testimony, but I do not understand your culture. Perhaps you can tell me if this is reasonable or not?''

''It's reasonable,'' Dagger answered.

''You believe she was *not* having an affair with this man? You believe her husband's suspicions were unfounded?''

''I believe that could well be the case. It's also quite possible the affair was real and she didn't want to lose the guy. I don't know either George or Harriet well enough to judge.''

''I could not get her to reveal the name of the man. She denies he's on this safari, but her refusal to divulge his name gives me pause.''

''She might merely be trying to protect an innocent man's reputation,'' Dagger answered. ''Let me think. She quarreled with George at the Masai Mara Lodge, out dancing on the terrace. She left and headed for their cabin, and George went into the bar for a drink or two. Twenty minutes later, he headed for the cabins himself, looking angry and determined. I thought then the fight might continue. Did they say anything about what they did that night?''

''She claims she went down to the cabin and that, when she was getting ready for bed, he came down. They both claim there was no fight, no further discussion of the matter."

"That's the only hostility I've seen between them on the trip," Dagger noted. "In fact, they looked pretty happy together when Richard was fawning over them. But Harriet hasn't been in a position on this trip to cheat, even if she wanted to, so George hasn't had reason to be jealous."

"You think the man George wanted transferred isn't on this tour?"

"If he were, I don't think George and Harriet would be getting along together at all."

"Yes, yes," Lumumba said, and made a note. "I agree."

"There's another point," Dagger went on. "Richard's two wristwatches. I presume you asked Samantha why he wore a watch on each wrist?"

Lumumba scowled. "I don't like that woman," he rumbled. "She keeps her body in shape, but her mind is a mess. I would not trust her mind."

Roxanne and I leaned a little more over the back of our seat. Dagger pretended no curiosity about that remark, but I saw the light come up in his eye. "Tell me about her mind," Dagger said, as if asking for a stock-market quotation.

"She pretends to be dumb, but she is *not* dumb. She's a very bright woman. I asked her about the two watches, why he wears two, and she says she 'thinks' the one on the right wrist, the better watch, was a 'gift.' From whom? I ask. She doesn't know. She can't even be sure it's a gift. It might have been a prize. A prize for what? She has no idea. Her husband doesn't talk to her, she doesn't talk to him.

" 'Why does he wear them both?' I ask. She doesn't know. The 'prize' watch, as she calls it, is more expensive, but he's had the digital a long time and it can do more things, give the day and date, serve as a stopwatch, that sort of thing. She believes he didn't want to give that one up."

"So why wear the other?" Dagger said. "Why not keep it in a drawer, or on the mantel—if it's a prize?"

"That was my question," Lumumba answered. "She said she didn't know. I asked if she didn't think he was displaying it for a purpose? She said, 'What purpose?' I said, 'Maybe to show it was appreciated. Maybe so the donor could see it?' She looked at me like I was crazy. She said, 'You think some *woman* on this safari gave him a watch and he's wearing it to show he cares? I dare you to name me some woman who'd give him *anything*!'" Lumumba turned to Dagger, and tapped his notes with his huge forefinger. "You see," he said, "what she's like? She's clever and she's dangerous."

Dagger nodded, his eyes hooded. He was absorbing and cataloguing all information that came his way. He spoke at last. "She wants us to believe the watch has nothing to do with the case."

"That's right," Lumumba grumbled. "The liar. Get this next one. I say to her how strange it is that that particular watch is missing from his body. Her answer is it's probably in some hippo's stomach, and if I don't want to accept that answer, she has another suggestion. It's lying in the grass near Richard's body, only we didn't find it."

Dagger did something he didn't often do. He got out and lighted a cigarette. Roxanne frowned her disapproval, but, as she'd confessed to me, she couldn't make him behave. I seldom saw him smoke, and only a little oftener did I see him have a drink. But there were the times I knew about, when, alone at night, when nobody was around, when unknown demons plagued him, he could down a liter of Scotch at a sitting and smoke two packs of cigarettes, each one down to the filter, and when he was through, no one would ever know. Not unless you watched him do it.

Now, he lighted a cigarette and I wondered, as Roxanne was wondering, whether it was the first of a string, or a single, solitary event. He said, "Tell me, Captain, if you will, what Samantha's alibi is for the night Richard died."

TWENTY-SIX

Monday, June 30

"HER STORY," Captain Lumumba said, "is that when she left the movie with her husband, he went to speak to the Gambles."

"The Gambles confirm that?"

"They say he tried to tell them how to handle me, that they shouldn't answer my questions."

"Which they obviously *did* answer."

"Gamble's a lawyer. He hardly needed advice from Richard. But I gather that was Richard's officious way, though he was weak-kneed enough when *I* questioned him."

"When his father died? What did he have to say?"

"He pretended great sorrow, alibied himself by saying he retired to his room about quarter past ten, showered, and was getting ready for bed when Duncan Hawley knocked on the door to tell him his father was dead. He didn't know what time that was."

Dagger said, "I went down to see the body at five minutes of eleven. It would have been about ten minutes after that. What about everybody else? Do you have time schedules?"

Lumumba nodded and thumbed through his notes. "Phineas kicked up a ruckus and went to his room around half past nine. The band had just started playing and was between numbers. Harriet Gamble says she went to her room shortly after ten. Say 10:05–10:20. George had two drinks in the bar and went to their room about half an hour later. Call it 10:30–10:35.

"When Richard went to his room, which he says was 10:15, Samantha stayed behind. She doesn't recall the time, so it's only his word."

"I remember it," Dagger answered. "That's about right."

"And somewhere in there," Lumumba read from his notes, "the porter delivered the bottle of poisoned liqueur."

"It was after that," Dagger said. "Maybe ten minutes later." To me he said, "Do you agree, James? I remember you remarked about it."

"Yes," I answered. "It was several minutes after Richard retired."

Lumumba stroked his chin. "Then Richard could not have made the phone call the lying manager said he made. There are no phones in the rooms."

"But we know *now* it wasn't Richard," said Dagger.

"I should have known then." Lumumba was hard on himself. He went on sourly. "As for the porter, he returned a couple of minutes later, having delivered the bottle. Then George went to his room, the Benedicts went to theirs, and finally, at about ten minutes to eleven, Duncan Hawley went down and found Phineas's body. Everyone else in the Cartwright group was still up on the terrace. Is that the reading you get?"

"That's the way I remember it," Dagger confirmed. "But I interrupted you. We were talking about *Samantha's* story of the night *Richard* died. Richard talked to the Gambles, and Samantha had two drinks with James and me. Then what?"

"She says you two walked her home, and the Benedicts were ahead of you. I place that time at 11:20."

Dagger agreed, and Lumumba went on. "Richard was there when she got in. They got into a bit of a quarrel, she says, and he left, claiming he was going to 'watch the hippos.' She believed he was going back to the bar. She went to bed and didn't know until the next morning that he hadn't come back."

"Can anybody else support any of this?"

Lumumba nodded. "Oh, yes, indeed. And that brings me to the most interesting tale of all. Jennifer Long's story! She and Lucy Children occupied the other half of the duplex. Now that she's dead, what she had to say may assume even *more* importance."

"Yes?" Dagger said, and though he didn't shift position, a gleam escaped his eye.

"They shared the same patio," Lumumba noted, "and there's only a wall dividing the two apartments. You can hear raised voices through the wall, and Jennifer heard the quarrel—not the words, but the voices. Her bed was against that wall and she heard the thud of something bumping on the other side. It woke her up. Then she heard their voices."

"What time was that?"

"Jennifer didn't know. She only half woke, heard the voices, and went back to sleep."

"And Lucy heard, too?"

The police captain shook his head. "Lucy was asleep on the other side of the room and, I understand, once she puts her head on a pillow, nothing can wake her. But," he went on, the note in his voice catching attention, "there's something Jennifer Long heard earlier which I think is even *more* important. Unfortunately, she had no corroboration and I don't know how honest she is, but I can't see any reason for her to lie, nor why or how she could make up something like this."

Even Dagger hung on his every word. Roxanne and I pressed closer.

"Jennifer and Lucy," Captain Lumumba continued, "returned to their cabin immediately after the movie. They walked with Peter Tower and invited him in for a drink, but he declined and went to his own cabin. That left Jennifer and Lucy alone. Figure they opened their door a bit after half past ten.

"In the cabin, so says Jennifer, while Lucy was in the bathroom getting ready for bed, she heard Richard arrive on the patio outside. She looked out the window and saw him clearly, and she insists no one else was with him. But she distinctly heard him say, and she swears he sounded upset, 'I must see Captain Lumumba immediately. It's important.' She swears nobody was with him, that he was talking to himself, but she equally swears that those were his exact words. 'I must see Captain Lumumba immediately. It's important.'"

Dagger's brow was deeply furrowed. "She recognized him and heard him say those particular words?" He paused to light a second cigarette. "Then what?"

Lumumba, who didn't smoke, shied slightly away and nodded. "She swore to those special words. She swore to seeing Richard on the patio. I queried her hard. I always query hard. It is my nature. 'Was someone else at hand, hidden in the shadows?' I demand. She says there wasn't, but she won't swear. I demand what did Richard do after she heard him make that statement, and she only says that he moved away, out of her sight."

"Which way?" Dagger asked automatically.

"All she would say was, 'into the shadows.' I demand of her, 'Then someone was with him!' She denies that vehemently. She claims he made that statement, as if to the sky, then moved away."

"Where did she think he was going?"

"She claimed she thought he was going to me. Why else would he say such a thing? But Richard Cartwright never came to see me. He stayed home and waited for Samantha. Why?"

Dagger was still frowning. "When Samantha got home, did Richard say anything to her about wanting to see you, or *not* wanting to see you, about that important something Jennifer claims he referred to?"

Lumumba shook his ponderous head. "Not a word. So either Jennifer's a liar or Richard changed his mind. Or Samantha's a liar and he *hadn't* changed his mind.

"So much for *that* strange feature," he went on. "The next strangeness is Richard's later quarrel with his wife. He walked out—to, as she puts it, 'see the hippos.' *She* thinks he's returning to the bar!

"But Richard Cartwright does not return to the bar, any more than he comes to see me." Lumumba shook his head at Dagger. "You people from America! I do not understand you at all. As a detective in Kenya, I am like a man walking on quicksand."

Colonel Dagger's eyes were deep and distant. He did not empathize with the police captain. He was having problems himself.

"Could Samantha tell you what time Richard left to, quote, go see the hippos?" he asked.

"She gives me stories like, 'Fifteen minutes? Half an hour?' I point out there's a big difference. 'I'm not a clock watcher,' she answers. That's more of her make-believe. Like her story about last night, when Jennifer Long was killed."

"What story?"

Lumumba made a face. "Do you know what she told me? She said, with Richard gone, she had the cabin to herself. So she tells me that, close to midnight, just before she turned in, she stepped out onto her patio in the dark to take in the night air. And, would you believe it, it was just at this moment that Jennifer was out and moving about? She claims she saw Jennifer, dressed as she'd been at dinner, walking a path, by herself, toward the farthest cabins. And do you know who occupied those farthest cabins? George and Harriet Gamble and Sylvia and Marshall Benedict.

"Now," Lumumba went on, holding up both hands, "who's going to believe a story like that? What on earth would Jennifer be going to any of them for? More than that, it's in the opposite direction from the crocodile's feeding ground where her body was ultimately dumped."

"That's hard to explain," Dagger conceded.

"So's her pretending she can't tell the difference between fifteen minutes and half an hour."

"At least we have her home with Richard by 11:30. The Benedicts were in their cabin, the Gambles in theirs, Duncan Hawley in his. Correct?"

"That's their claim. Duncan doesn't have anybody to vouch for him. The others are husbands and wives and might be covering for each other."

"None of them saw anything?"

"So they swear."

"That leaves Peter Tower. What about him?"

"Tower returned to his cabin with Lucy and Jennifer, declining to drink with them. That would be about 10:30. He says he reached his door the same time Lucy and Jennifer reached theirs and he saw Richard Cartwright coming along the walk about fifty feet away. He was passing under one of the lamps they have along the path, and he was heading for his own cabin. Behind him, Peter said, fifty feet farther back, someone else was coming along the path, a man, he thinks, but the figure was too far away and not under the light. That's all he could report seeing and hearing, except that he poured himself a drink and was getting ready for bed when he thought he heard Neville on the patio and went to let him in, but it was George and Harriet, who had the other half of the duplex.''

"Who could have been the figure on the path behind Richard?" Dagger asked.

"Duncan Hawley. Nobody else could have been on the path at that time. All the others are accounted for. But Duncan swears he didn't see *anyone*. And Lucy and Jennifer didn't see Richard, but they were farther away and were entering their cabin.''

Dagger dismissed the apparent contradiction. "Peter saw Richard, and maybe Duncan Hawley. And he met the Gambles when they arrived. What else did he do?"

"Went to bed, he said. After he got to bed, he claims he could hear the Gambles having words—not the words, but the voices. They deny, on the other hand, that they were quarreling.''

"That brings us to Neville Street," Dagger said, and turned to Roxanne with a hard look. "You and Neville closed up the bar that night, didn't you? What time was that?"

"Oh dear, Papa," she said. "Do you mean when the bar closed or when Neville dropped me off at my quarters?"

The colonel reddened for a moment. He went on in a softer, more tenuous voice. "Let's talk about when and where you said good night.''

"Oh," she said, smiling at him with deep affection, "we said good night on my doorstep. At about—half past twelve." She gave him her quixotic look and patted his hand, which was gripping the back of our seats. "All very proper, Papa. I did let him kiss me good night, but, if I'm not mistaken, that's the least of what you did with the girls you courted."

"Neville Street is not courting you," Colonel Dagger announced. "And neither is that Peter Tower."

"Oh dear," Roxanne answered, giving her father a huge, innocent, blue-eyed stare. "Are you suggesting their intentions aren't honorable?"

"Sometimes," Colonel Dagger answered, "I wonder why fathers have daughters. Sons are curse enough. Thank you, my darling Roxanne. May we return to the time schedule? This rat Neville Street kissed you good night on your patio at half past twelve?"

Roxanne darted a sly glance my way and said, "I wasn't really paying attention to the time, Papa. That's only a guess. I was only interested in the kiss."

Colonel Dagger was having difficulty keeping his personal antipathy for young Cartwright bachelors from interfering with his analysis of the case. He got out from under by turning to the police captain and saying testily, "What did Neville see and hear, and the Benedicts? Sometime during the night Richard was killed and dumped over the wall. Is everybody alibied? Is everyone deaf, dumb, and blind? What's the story? Are they all in cahoots?"

"Now you know what I'm up against," Lumumba answered. "Neville claims Peter was asleep when he came in. He claims he got into bed and read the Bible for fifteen minutes, then went to sleep himself."

"The Bible!" the colonel exploded.

"He claims he does it every night. It brings him peace."

"What kind of guys do you go out with?" Dagger demanded of Roxanne.

Lumumba answered for her. "There are those, Colonel, people of the *Christian* faith, who find the words of the Bible to be of great value."

Roxanne gave the captain a smile and a sigh. "You have to forgive my father," she said. "The last time he was in a church was for his mother's funeral. If he'd had to get married in church, he'd have three less ex-wives than he does now."

TWENTY-SEVEN

Monday, June 30

WE PASSED THROUGH the village of Nanyuki on the edge of the equator just before 12:00 and the vans stopped for a tea break at the Silverbeck Hotel, which was exactly on the equator, some rooms on one side, some on the other. Tea and cakes were served on a sun-drenched patio at metal tables shielded by umbrellas, and Colonel Dagger hosted Captain Lumumba, Roxanne, our driver Amram Kitanyi, and me. Amram, who was twenty-eight, married, and of long experience in safari travel, was usually taciturn and stuck strictly to the subject of the birds and animals about which he knew so much. Not once, since his dire prediction after the incident at the baboon park, had he expressed himself on the deaths and gloom that had laid such a pall over this particular safari.

Here, however, in the intimate atmosphere we created, he did open up a little. He'd experienced many things on his safari tours, he told us; people getting sick, people getting injured—the Italian tourist who dropped his camera into a clear hot spring and thrust his hand in after it, forgetting the water was two hundred degrees. The skin on his hand and forearm was taken right off, Amram said, and that poor tourist spent the rest of the tour in the hospital and a good deal longer besides.

There were the funny things, he said, and the crazy things, and the dangerous things—an ill-tempered elephant forcing vans into a quick retreat at the threat of a charge, and

God help the tourists if the engines didn't start. Mostly, though, elephants were benign creatures. They had nothing to be afraid of, even lions couldn't hurt them. All they wanted to do was graze and gouge bark off trees with their tusks. You could tell whether an elephant was left-tusked or right-tusked according to which was shorter and more broken.

But, Amram confessed, never had he been on such a safari as ours. Never before had a tourist died on safari, let alone *three*! Never before had such a cloud of doom hung over a group of tourists. Even the bird watchers, excepting, of course, the indefatigable Sidney Leggett, had lost interest in the purpose of the trip.

"I feel useless," he confessed. "All of us drivers feel useless. What can we show you, what can we do for you? Nobody cares. Everybody wonders who will be the next to die. You look into each other's faces, not out at our parks."

"There are problems," Lumumba admitted.

"There are," Amram agreed. "Perhaps we should skip Crestview Lodge and return at once to Nairobi? Perhaps we should end the tour?"

Lumumba shook his head. He'd structured his investigation to the tour's itinerary and the need to produce a killer before its end. He couldn't afford to shorten his time. Nor was he a man easily able to change tactics or improvise. Nor, I suspected, would his superiors allow it.

Jennifer's death had forced him to ask Dagger for help, the excuse being that Dagger was better able to understand the white man's mentality. Meanwhile, however, he had to pursue the original plan—solve the murders without interrupting the tour. See that the tourists get their money's worth. Don't damage Kenyan tourism by canceling or shortchanging!

Through hell or high water, I suspected, Lumumba would
see the safari to its ultimate conclusion. At the same time,
he was required to catch the killer. These were, I guessed, the
orders he'd been given from above, and no excuse would
satisfy his superiors if he failed.

I felt for him, for I sensed a dedicated man given a task he
could not accomplish. In this effort to fulfill his mission,
he'd even turned to a white man for help. Though he gave
no sign, I tasted the bitter gall that lay in his spleen.

WE GOT UNDER WAY again at 12:20, crossed the equator
heading south, and, with a brief stop at a curio shop for
souvenirs, arrived at Crestview Lodge at half past one.

Crestview, built beside a water hole, was the climax of the
tour, offering guests a view of all the animals which came to
drink.

Dagger and I lucked out, getting a room where the balcony overlooked the water hole, with Roxanne and Lise on
our left, and the Benedicts on our right. Given our balcon-
ies, we didn't have to go to the lounge or the lodge roof to
watch the activity.

One can say we lucked out, except that nobody, other
than Sidney Leggett, cared any more about seeing animals
or traveling in vans. Nobody—always excepting old Leggett—talked about anything except Jennifer's death and
who was the monster in our midst.

Half our people didn't turn up for lunch and throughout
the afternoon, the Cartwright survivors roamed aimlessly,
stayed in their rooms, or patronized the bar. Outside, some
forty cape buffalo monopolized the water hole, joined by
small antelope, an oryx, and a couple of forest hogs, but
nobody, except maybe me, noticed.

Dagger stayed in our room all afternoon. He wanted to be
alone, he said, so I circulated, hoping to encounter Rox-

anne since Neville and Peter weren't in evidence. But she wasn't in evidence, either. I saw Marshall Benedict sitting at the lounge window by himself, staring sightlessly at the mass of cape buffalo.

"Interesting, aren't they?" I remarked, coming up beside him, and he turned glassy eyes in my direction. "What is?"

I indicated where he'd been looking. "The cape buffalo."

"Oh." He turned and saw them for the first time. "Yes, very interesting."

"Where's Sylvia?"

"In the room. She's not feeling well."

"I noticed she wasn't here for lunch. Is it serious?"

"Ptomaine, I think. Something she had for breakfast. She's very sick."

I wondered why, if she were as sick as he claimed, he wasn't with her. "Does she need a doctor?"

"It's indigestion," he returned. "Something she ate. Nobody can do anything. Her system has to purge itself."

"You're sure it's *only* that?"

He gave me a startled look. "What do you mean?"

"I mean, she hasn't been *poisoned*, has she? It's not cyanide, is it?"

The big, burly man was on his feet, taller than I and twice as broad. "Are you suggesting there's something deliberate about this?"

I backed off. "I don't know a thing. I'm just edgy. The way people are dying on this trip, I don't know what's going to happen to whom, next."

"But Sylvia? Nobody'd want to hurt Sylvia!" The disbelief in his face was overshadowed by alarm.

"And who'd want to hurt *Jennifer*?"

"I'd better look in on her," Marshall said, and hurried away.

I wish I could tell you where everybody was at every moment that afternoon, but I wasn't Dagger. I didn't have his qualities of observation that pinpointed everybody's location from moment to moment. I didn't have the mental clock that ticked in his mind.

I saw Peter at one time, Neville at another, the Gambles standing together, but not relating, at still another. And Lucy Children, sitting at a table alone, with a big whiskey sour in front of her, dabbing at her eyes with a handkerchief.

Close to dinnertime, I dared return to the room and found it dense with cigarette smoke, the colonel propped on his bed, a notepad in hand, an ashtray overflowing with cigarette butts, and a half-empty bottle of Scotch at his elbow.

He looked up somberly at my entrance. "Don't worry," he said, indicating the Scotch bottle and small tumbler beside it, "I'm not drunk. As you can see, half the bottle's left." He did not mention the cigarette smoke that filled the room, despite the open door to the tiny balcony.

"What've you been doing?"

His was a painful smile, and he shook his head. "You know something, James?" he answered. "The pieces don't fit together. I can't make the pieces fit together."

I'd been thinking the way Captain Lumumba'd been thinking, that bringing the colonel into the case would provide a solution. But now he was saying he couldn't solve it, either. I experienced a sinking feeling. If he couldn't, and Captain Lumumba couldn't, what was going to happen?

"Sylvia Benedict's very ill," I told him. "Marshall thinks it's something she ate at breakfast. I've been wondering if it might not be cyanide again."

"Cyanide?" He frowned. "Where could it come from?"

I shook my head. "Who knows where our drug addicts get crack?"

"James," Dagger said, rising from the bed, "all you do is make an impossible puzzle even *more* impossible." He chucked his notebook aside, smiled at me, and said, "It's dinnertime and I think we should eat. I forgot to have lunch."

TWENTY-EIGHT

Monday, June 30

IF CAPTAIN LUMUMBA and Colonel Dagger were at their wits' end, and the members of the safari group were tormented by fear and worry over the commission of three murders on the safari tour, bedlam broke loose after dinner at the discovery of a fourth!

Dinner itself was a dismal meal. The tragedies had driven wedges between friends and acquaintances. The bird watchers clung together like derelict sailors, shunning the rest of us, not even speaking when spoken to.

Lumumba, Dagger, Roxanne, and I ate together, Roxanne, for once, not being courted by the Cartwright skirt-chasers, Peter Tower and Neville Street.

No one seemed to want to make up to anybody. It was every man for himself now. Eyes were everywhere. Who had come in? Who sat with whom?

Marshall Benedict entered alone and ate alone. Word of Sylvia's illness had circulated and nobody wanted to be near him. Nobody wanted to ask how she was.

Except Lumumba. He went over, had words, and returned with Marshall's report: Sylvia was still ailing, but a doctor had seen her and claimed it was digestive upset. Though poison was supposedly not involved, Marshall was still being treated as a pariah.

At our table, Dagger was moody and fretful, Roxanne silent. Lumumba watched the room and muttered. I tried to be watchful and again and again went over the list of Cart-

wright people among the diners: Duncan Hawley, Peter
Tower, Neville Street, Marshall Benedict, George and Har-
riet Gamble. Who among them had killed three people?
Who was going to kill again?

The fear of a fourth victim hung over the room like a pall.
I wondered why there should be such ominous foreboding.
Was there a feeling that the job had not yet been done, that
it would take *four* to complete it?

Lumumba and Dagger shared that tense expectancy as
well. Their eyes were everywhere and they ate in bits and
pieces, scarcely aware of what they were doing.

In time the meal was finished. Dessert and coffee were
served and Lumumba, scowling, suddenly leaned close to
Dagger. "Where's Samantha?" he growled in low tones.

"Not here yet," Dagger replied in an equally quiet voice.

"I think we ought to find out why."

Dagger nodded. "She should have been here by now."

Together they got up. "You sit," Dagger commanded
Roxanne and me. "Finish your dessert and coffee."

"You think something's happened to her?" Roxanne
asked.

Dagger shook his head. "No. We're just going to check.
But you stay here. If anybody asks, we've gone to see the
manager."

They were off, and Roxanne turned to me. "For once,
I'm scared."

"You think something's happened to Samantha? Sylvia's the one who's sick."

"I'm scared because Captain Lumumba and my father
see things I don't see, and know things I don't know.
They're worried because Samantha hasn't come to dinner.
That makes *me* worry!"

"It's only just dark," I reassured her. "Nothing can have happened. All the murders were done at night. Late at night."

"I don't care what's happened when," she answered. "When my father and that police captain decide to investigate something, I know it's something bad. I feel it in my bones. Maybe it's because I'm my father's daughter, but I get his vibrations."

We ate cherry cobbler and sipped coffee in silence, poised to field questions from the other diners, for the eyes of everyone turned the moment Dagger and Lumumba rose from the table and never left the pair until they were gone from the room. After that, the eyes were on Roxanne and me, projecting suspicious, worried, nervous stares which we bowed our heads to avoid. But no one—not a single person—dared to leave his own haven and come ask us where the captain and the colonel had gone. It was as if they feared the answer, or had guessed the answer.

What galvanized the morbid group was the sound of inordinate activity in the outside halls, a hurrying and scurrying. At the first untoward sounds, the diners forgot their cherry cobbler and coffee and rose as one in a panicked race to the source of the commotion.

By the time Roxanne and I reached the crowd in the doorway, the rumor was circulating so loudly that we could have heard it back at the table: Samantha Cartwright had been found dead on her bed, fully clothed and strangled.

Other rumors were also circulating, rumors that turned Roxanne's face pale and struck fear even to my own heart. The question was, who could have gained entrance? Samantha's door was locked. It had taken the manager's key to open it.

And how else could anyone have gotten in?

Via the balcony door was the only other possibility. But
each balcony had a partition that would have to be circum-
vented, and all were plainly visible from the lounge. No sane
person could hope to reach Samantha by balcony unde-
tected.

Captain Lumumba appeared, a sick look in his eyes, a
look that almost said he'd rather be dead. Who could blame
him? Three additional murders taking place under his nose
while he was trying to solve the first? He'd even turned to
Colonel Dagger for help and not only had the colonel not
helped, the carnage continued. What would he do now?

The colonel was with him, discreetly a step behind. Lumumba had not yet cast him aside as a useless reed. Perhaps even a useless reed was better than standing entirely
alone.

The tour group was ordered to remain together in the
lobby while Captain Lumumba, this time assisted by Colonel Dagger, interrogated each member individually in the
manager's office. The order smacked of numerous earlier
such orders by Lumumba, and numerous earlier inquisi-
tions through which he had sought: first, to discover who
had poisoned Phineas Cartwright; second, who had broken Richard's skull and thrown him to the hippos; third,
who had strangled Jennifer and fed her to the crocodiles;
and now, fourth, who had entered Samantha's room sometime during the afternoon and squeezed the life out of an
athletic, capable, robust woman without allowing her the
chance to scream.

My turn with them was brief. Lumumba was behind the
manager's desk, a now familiar position, with Dagger in a
chair to the side, posing as a spectator. But Dagger's eyes
were as soul-searching as Lumumba's and he couldn't hide
the fact. Dagger could file his nails while Lumumba questioned; he could study the shine on his shoes, on my shoes,

the color of the paint on the walls, but when I sat before
Captain Lumumba and watched Colonel Dagger out of the
corner of my eye, I thought that, were I the murderer, I'd be
more afraid of the colonel than the captain.

But I wasn't the murderer. I was a token testator. Both
knew I had nothing to do with the killings and was merely
going through the motions for the benefit of the other suspects. Of course, they did want to know what I might have
seen or heard, but I doubt they expected any worthwhile
information from anyone. In fact, I was certain they
wouldn't get any. Whoever had been committing these horrible crimes either had a gift for covering *his* tracks (I no
longer believed it could possibly be a *her*) or had been born
beloved by gods who smiled fondly upon his endeavors.

I was sent away quickly and went out to Roxanne, who
was being almost totally ignored by Neville and Peter. Both
of them, at that moment, looked more interested in self-
preservation than species preservation and more concerned
with snowing the authorities as to the pure white innocence
of their nature than in snowing a nearby beautiful female as
to the red-hot depths of their passion.

I wished Roxanne could read their evil intentions as
readily as I, but she remained sublimely oblivious, only
concerned with how much her father could help Captain
Lumumba end those awful tragedies.

And what would happen next?

On the morrow we were scheduled to return to the Sabrina Hotel in Nairobi and, the next day, take off for home.

But would that happen, with a murderer running loose?

WHEN HE HAD COMPLETED his interrogations, Captain Lumumba gave us orders. We would sleep as best we could on
the chairs, couches, and floor of the lobby with police
standing guard. Persons using the facilities would be ac-

companied by a guard who would wait outside. No one was
to be alone at any time. First thing in the morning, our vans
would return us to our hotel in Nairobi where we would be
under similar protection. "No one else will die," the captain said. "That is a promise."

There was useless grumbling as we tourists bedded down
for an uncomfortable night in the lounge. What irked me,
in addition, was the universal police tactic of demanding
information, but never giving any. And I had so many
questions. When had Samantha been killed? Had there been
a struggle? Were there any clues? What had been done with
her body? What would be done with us back in Nairobi?
And had they noted that the apparently random murders
had succeeded in wiping out everyone in the Cartwright
family?

Lumumba wasn't talking, however, and I found the colonel equally reticent. He was on the side of the police now
and behaving just like *them*.

TWENTY-NINE

Tuesday, July 1

THE MORNING SUN was brilliant in a cloudless sky and the peak of nearby Mount Kenya, 17,208 feet high, shrouded yesterday by clouds, stood stark and gray, whitened by snow in its shaded areas, against its blue backdrop. Around the water hole was a mixture of elephants and cape buffalo. It was the first time anybody had noticed the water hole after Samantha's murder.

Two of Lumumba's khaki-clad policemen shepherded us weary, uncomfortable, uneasy, but also excited tourists into the dining hall for breakfast. Oh yes, there was excitement, the kind brought on by shared travail, the thought of what stories we'd have to tell when we got home from all this! We felt safe with Lumumba's police on guard, with a bright sun above, being herded everywhere in a bunch.

Over breakfast, which Roxanne and I shared with Lumumba and the colonel, Lumumba grudingly gave forth some details about Samantha's murder. No one had seen the killer enter Samantha's room, either by door or balcony. Presumably, since the hallway was generally empty, the killer had entered through the door. The guess was she'd answered a knock and let him in, not anticipating her fate.

I said, "You agree, then, that it's a *he*?"

"It's a turn of phrase," Lumumba answered. "The colonel and I don't rule out any possibility."

He was considering Colonel Dagger as a co-worker now— despite their failure to make progress or prevent Samantha's murder! I caught their exchange of glances and the hate was gone from the captain's eyes. When two people have need of each other, racial and cultural differences lose their meaning, let alone their importance.

"Was there a struggle? Was there an outcry?"

Lumumba, with a nod from the colonel, confided that no one had seen or heard a sound, but few people were in their rooms at the time. Yes, there *had* been a struggle. The bed and Samantha's clothes were mussed and wrinkled. The killing took place between three and six—after lunch and before dinner—but could not be pinpointed closer without an autopsy, which was being performed today in Nairobi. None of the safari members, except Sylvia Benedict who'd been in bed, could alibi himself for the whole three hours. That included the colonel, Roxanne, and me.

I said that Colonel Dagger was alibied. Like Sylvia, he'd spent the afternoon in his room.

"That is not an alibi," Lumumba answered, and Dagger agreed. "That's only where you *think* I spent the afternoon. There's no proof."

"What you're telling me," I said in dismay, "is that you've got *nothing* to go on? Four murders, and you have nothing?" Somehow I'd expected more from the colonel. I'd thought when he entered the case it was the Marines to the rescue. But that was, I realized, asking rather much. Perhaps I'd idolized him from afar and clothed him in the garb of Supersleuth. It wasn't his fault if he couldn't live up to the image.

"Not 'nothing,'" Lumumba answered. "The colonel and I have reached certain conclusions about the case. One is that someone in the tour group is so desperate he kills in the most reckless situations."

"A lunatic," I said. "But I can't detect lunacy in anyone's eyes."

"Nor do we," Lumumba acknowledged. "On that point, we agree."

"So the killer is desperate," I protested. "That should be obvious to the most innocent bystander. Do you have nothing else?"

It was Dagger who answered, his manner thoughtful. "There are a lot of pieces, James," he said, "pieces I have gone over with the captain. They don't fit together. Captain Lumumba and I have been trying to *make* them fit, but they won't."

"You mean," I said, "there are pieces missing?"

"No," Dagger answered. "No missing pieces. It's just that the ones we've got won't mesh."

"There are liars in *your* midst," Lumumba replied, then corrected himself. "In the *group*," he amended. "Among the *Cartwright* tourists. That's why the pieces won't mesh."

"There are always liars," Dagger agreed. "And the pieces won't mesh until we find out what lies won't let them mesh."

THE FOUR VANS got under way on the final leg of the safari trip at half past nine that morning. Ours, of course, was driven by Amram and contained the Lumumba-Dagger-Roxanne-James Addison quartet, and we traveled mostly in silence. Amram didn't point out a single bird. No one was quicker than he to sense the mood of his vanload.

Lumumba and Dagger, side by side on the middle seat, sat in thought, with one occasionally turning to the other with an idea or to test a theory. Lumumba would say, "Why would Richard, talking to himself, claim he had to come see me about something important—when I was ready to arrest him for murder—and never show up?"

"Why would Jennifer tell you such a story?"

"She's lying."

"But why?"

And Lumumba would shake his head and go back into thought.

Or Dagger would say, "Richard's body was found near the camel path, a long way from the wall. Could it have been put there by the killer, or was it wrestled there by angry hippos?"

"If the killer had tried to deposit the body where we found it, the hippos would have slaughtered him. We have to accept that the hippos mauled the body from the wall to that point. They don't like foreign objects in their territory."

"Do you think, Captain, Richard could have lost his wristwatch through being mauled?"

"It's possible. Anything's possible. It might right now be lying somewhere in the grass."

"But you won't make me believe it."

"You won't make me either."

THE VANS ARRIVED BACK at the Nairobi Sabrina Hotel at 12:30 and we all were immediately taken in for lunch. Even here, Lumumba's minions were in charge, and if you wanted to go to the bathroom, you had to be accompanied by one of his men. We were given special stares by the other residents of the hotel, and I wondered what our sleeping arrangements would be this night. And what would happen on the morrow when, that evening, we were supposed to fly back to the United States?

At lunch, Captain Lumumba announced that our group would pay a visit, en toto, to the baboon park. Ordinarily, it would have been a free afternoon for shopping and relaxing and doing what we chose. Not now, however. The group was to stay together, forever under Lumumba's watchful eye. Like it or not, we were to revisit the baboon park.

The vans took us there at two o'clock and we were freed to stroll along the paths and feed bread and rolls to the baboons under the watchful eyes of Lumumba's police. Lumumba and Dagger stayed together at the end of the group, watching and murmuring, and I stayed close. I'd seen enough baboons and I sensed something was about to explode. Dagger and the captain were where it all was at.

Meanwhile, the safari tourists, feeling safely shepherded, began to relax. Guards slowly dropped and they resorted to form. Peter Tower once again won Roxanne away from Neville Street and Neville was left sulking on the fringes, casting angry glares at his roommate. Lucy Children, companionless, wandered aimlessly. George and Harriet Gamble walked apart like strangers, except that Harriet moved like a free soul, and George was restrained, moving always with one jealous eye on his wife, as if he expected a stranger to make a move on her—almost as if this was what he was waiting for.

Sylvia was present, wan and unhappy, attending the park tour only because she was physically able. Nobody wanted to be there, but it was one way Lumumba could keep us all under his wing without holding us under house arrest as well.

Marshall, Sylvia's big, lumbering husband, capable of smothering her merely by taking her in his arms, hovered around her, pleased that she was ambulatory again. They really *did* seem to like each other.

And Duncan Hawley? It was not his bag. I didn't think any of it was his bag and wondered why he'd come. Maybe because Phineas had *told* him to?

We spread out along the path, the others ahead, Dagger and Lumumba at the rear, watching their flock, and me adjacent, watching them.

AND THEN IT HAPPENED. Colonel Dagger put a hand on
Captain Lumumba's arm. "I've got it," he said. "I think I
know the key. Get Harriet Gamble over here."

Lumumba didn't even question. He signaled one of his
men and pointed. In a moment, a querying Harriet was on
hand, her husband turning to stare suspiciously, but hesi-
tating to follow. George watched her like the proverbial
hawk but wasn't sure he wanted to chase after her and run
afoul of Lumumba.

"Yes?" Harriet asked, a police escort at her side, her
unsuspecting eyes moving from Lumumba's face to Dagger's. "What do you want?"

It was Dagger who answered. "Harriet," he said, "what
was Richard after when he came to see you? A drink? Sex?
A chance to talk?"

"What are you talking about?" She stared at him, but
shivered.

"That first night," Dagger went on. "At the Masai Mara.
Richard came to see you. Why?"

"But you're crazy! Nobody came to see me. I went to my
quarters and, after a while, George came down, too. He'll
tell you. Richard wasn't with me. Nobody was."

"George has said different," Dagger told her. "Do you
want me to call him over?"

Harriet blanched. It was all Dagger needed. "I don't want
to call George," he said. "I want *your* story. I've already got
his!"

Harriet looked ready to cry. "It's no different. Nothing
happened. I swear to you. It's what I told George. What he
told you was the honest truth!"

"Tell it to me in your own words," Dagger answered.
"Why did Richard come? What did he want?"

Harriet put both hands on Dagger's sleeve. "Please,
Colonel." She glanced once at Lumumba. "Here's what

happened—honest. I was quarreling with George on the dance floor. It was about his jealousies. About a divorce. And I left him and went to the room.

"And five minutes later, there's a knock on the door and Richard's standing there—not really drunk, but keyed up. And he pushed his way in and wanted to make love to me. I told him he was crazy, but he said he'd discovered his wife was cheating on him and he gave me some mishmash about being entitled to even the score. I don't even think the guy had ever cheated on his wife before. He didn't know the first way to go about it. All he's spent his life doing was trying to please his father. And then he discovers his wife's been unfaithful—hell, he probably hadn't been to bed with her for two years worrying about tomorrow at the office—and now he was trying to get even—and with me!

"I tried to get him out of there and told him what George would do if he should come home. And then George *did* come home. And all I could think of was, 'Oh, God.'

"I don't know how drunk Richard was when he tried, in his inept way, to seduce me, but once George arrived, he went into a panic. He promised us anything if we'd just keep still about it! Anything, anything! Even Jealous George knew the guy was harmless and went along. So we let the story stand that Richard had gone to his cabin, as I'd gone to mine, and George came down a few minutes later and would back it." Then Harriet said to Dagger, "Who told you Richard hadn't gone to his cabin? How did you know he came to me?"

Colonel Dagger didn't answer. He dismissed her, saying he'd talk to her later.

When she left, a baffled expression on her face, Captain Lumumba stared wide-eyed at Dagger. "How did you *know* this—that Richard went to Harriet's cabin instead of his own?"

"I didn't," Dagger answered. "I deduced it."

"Deduced it?"

"Captain, it's the *only* explanation that would fit the pieces together!"

Lumumba shook his head in a despair that approached defeat. "How can a police detective in Kenya understand the minds of the tourists who come to his country? What enabled you to deduce it? How did you deduce it? Tell me about the mind of the white man."

THIRTY

Tuesday, July 1

COLONEL DAGGER spoke intensely and quietly to Captain Lumumba, while I listened. "Back at the Masai Mara, before you were involved," he told the captain, "Phineas Cartwright was poisoned. Let us pay attention to the time schedule. Phineas kicked up a fuss about nine-thirty and went to his quarters.

"Let's say I want to kill Phineas with a bottle of poisoned liqueur. Would I not send it to him post haste? Should he not receive it within the next ten minutes? This does not happen.

"Next, about ten after ten, Harriet has words with her husband. She retires to their quarters and he goes to the bar for twenty to twenty-five minutes, then follows after. Meanwhile, five minutes after Harriet departs, Richard Cartwright fights with Samantha and takes off to *his* room. And, less than *ten* minutes later, a poisoned bottle is delivered.

"Wouldn't you assume, given that scenario, that the bottle was meant for Richard? I certainly did!

"But Phineas got it, and I appeared to be mistaken since Richard claimed to have been in his quarters the whole time and Harriet supported him by saying she was alone in hers, and everybody else was up on the terrace. And it would stretch the imagination too far to believe the porter, delivering a bottle to Richard Cartwright in cabin 3, would deliver it instead to Phineas Cartwright in cabin 1.

"So I had to accept—everybody had to accept—that Phineas was the intended victim.

"But that made a mess out of everything. What's the motive for killing father and son? There'd have to be a connection. Why send Phineas a rare and expensive liqueur when his son says he wouldn't know the difference? The son knew the difference all right."

Dagger shook his head. "Remove Phineas from the case and everything else fitted. Leave him in, and nothing worked. But, as I say, it was too farfetched to believe he got the bottle by mistake with Richard right next door.

"That got me thinking, finally, about a way in which a messenger, carrying a bottle to a Mr. Cartwright in cabin no. 3 might deliver it, instead, to Mr. Cartwright in cabin no. 1.

"The one possibility would be if cabin no. 3 was dark and unoccupied. Then the messenger, eager to dispense his duties, not caring which Mr. Cartwright he could unload his burden upon, might dump it into Phineas's lap. And if Phineas got the poison, we both know the manager at the Masai Mara wouldn't voluntarily tell you it was supposed to go to Richard."

Lumumba nodded and ground his teeth.

"But," Dagger continued, "if Richard's cabin were dark and unoccupied, where could he have gone? It would have to be Harriet's cabin, she being the only other person down there. If *that* had happened, everything else could be explained. If it hadn't, nothing could. So I worked on that premise and got her to admit Richard had been there. And the rest of what she said verified the rest of my conclusions."

"What are they?" Lumumba and I wanted to know.

"Start with Richard and Samantha. Richard is under his father's thumb. He's a slave to the office. He doesn't chase women, he doesn't know how, he doesn't have time. When he, to 'get even' with Samantha, tries to make a pass at Harriet, he proves totally inept.

"But what about Samantha? She's left alone all the time. So she's into golf, swimming, tennis. So it wouldn't be surprising if she were into men as well. It might even be expected. And judging by the hate displayed between them, I'd suspect Richard knew about it—a fact Harriet now confirms.

"Why wouldn't he have started divorce proceedings? Because he only just found out about it—just before the safari started. According to Lucy, Samantha and Richard got along politely, if not lovingly, before the trip. On the trip he's dripping venom. Let's suggest that as soon as the trip is over, he's going to kick Samantha out, and destroy the lover as well.

"Does he know who the lover is? No. Why? Because the lover was able to grab his clothes and flee in time when Richard arrived home unexpectedly."

"How can you know this?" Lumumba said, mystified.

"I don't know it, Captain, I assure you. I only say this because it's the only way the pieces fit.

"The way I have to conclude things happened is that Richard came home, found his wife in the bedroom, her lover gone. He wouldn't even have known there'd been a lover, except the lover left a piece of evidence behind—his wristwatch.

"Innocent Richard is now outraged. He's going to throw out his wife and ruin her lover as soon as he can trace the wristwatch, which he's going to do as soon as the safari's over. Meanwhile, for safe-keeping, he wears the watch on his right wrist."

"You deduced all this?" Lumumba said in awe.

"There's no other way to explain what happened," Dagger answered. "To kill Richard in Kenya is an act of desperation. The threat of ruin seems to me the only threat powerful enough to produce such desperation. I have to assume Samantha told her lover what Richard planned and they both decided he must never return from Africa. Richard didn't know the identity of the lover. What he also didn't know was that the lover happened to be coming on the safari.

"The lover, who's traveled before, knows he can sneak cyanide through customs without any trouble. Samantha knows Richard's favorite liqueur—that was one mistake they made, tipping Richard off by buying his favorite.

"They have it delivered to him but his father gets it instead. The father dies and his body is shipped home. Now here's something interesting. Why didn't Richard and Samantha go home, too? That would be the logical procedure. But Samantha would do her damnedest to persuade Richard to stay in Africa. He must not return to the States alive.

"And what would allow him to be persuaded? The need to keep George and Harriet quiet about the pass he made. He wouldn't be able to destroy Samantha as effectively as he'd like if that came out. He wants to buy their silence by promising them, as new head of the company, all sorts of goodies.

"So back they come, and into the case *you* come. You announce that Phineas was poisoned by his favorite liqueur. Richard scoffs at that to James and me, then goes to talk to the Gambles—not to tell them how to deal with you, but to ensure that they don't tell you about the pass he made. Then he returns to his cabin while Samantha is having drinks with James and me.

"Meanwhile, the lover is lying in wait, armed with a large rock, and meets Richard on his patio. And it's just at that moment it dawns on Richard, who isn't the fastest thinker in the world, the Père Javineau liqueur was *his* favorite, and could it possibly be that the poison was meant for *him*? That frightens him and he's ready to run to you with the information, but the lover gets him off in the shadows, bashes in his head, gets rid of the wristwatch, throws it into the woods or something, and either dumps Richard's body over the wall or, if he needs help, leaves him behind the cabin and waits for Samantha.

"When she arrives, she and the lover fake a squabble to make Jennifer, next door, think he's Richard and still alive—at least forty-five minutes after Richard's already dead. Then they dump his body, if it hasn't already been done, and go to their cabins.

"Meanwhile, Jennifer had seen the lover approach Richard on the patio—"

"Lying Americans!" Lumumba rumbled. "She *swore* she hadn't."

"She *had* to have. Otherwise she'd still be alive."

"She witnessed the murder and the lover knew it?"

"No. Otherwise she would've told. She'd've been too frightened not to. What I think happened is she saw the guy with Richard but didn't suspect he was the killer because she thought she heard Richard quarreling with Samantha later. But she thought this man would prefer that nobody knew he was one of the last people to see Richard alive. She thought he might be grateful to her if she didn't mention his name."

"What would that do for her?"

"Judging from her hunger, I'd guess she believed that he, in his gratitude, might be persuaded to show an interest in her, court her a little, maybe even take her to bed, if what Lucy claims about her is true. And, of course, if he refused to be nice to her, she could suddenly remember she *did* see someone with Richard after all."

"Lying Americans," Lumumba growled again.

"The lover, of course, was very appreciative of her not mentioning his name. He made a secret date with her for that very evening and made sure she wouldn't *ever* mention his name by throwing her to the crocodiles. And, of course, Samantha helped out by telling you she saw Jennifer heading toward the Gambles' and Benedicts' cottages at midnight, probably a good hour after she was already dead."

Lumumba grumbled, "I told you she was a dangerous woman."

"And a problem as well."

"Samantha?"

Dagger nodded. "It's interesting about Samantha. Why didn't she go back to the States with her dead husband? That's the natural thing to do.

"Instead, back she comes to the tour group offering the feeblest of excuses. She wanted to postpone misery! The real reason, I think, was jealousy. She and her lover had committed three murders together and she thought that bound them forever. She'd alibied him, he'd alibied her—it made them inseparable. Yet there he was, making a big play for my daughter, and it made her furious." Dagger gestured up the walk to where Peter was strolling with Roxanne, cradling her arm tight against him. "See, there he is making his play right now, only he doesn't have to hold back any longer."

Dagger sighed. "Did you happen to notice, Captain," he said, "how Peter came on to Roxanne like gangbusters whenever Samantha's back was turned, and backed off and gave Neville a chance when Samantha was around? I think that's what brought Samantha back. She didn't want to leave Peter around Roxanne unattended.

"Samantha probably expected marriage when things quieted down, even if Peter was several years her junior. But Peter wasn't seducing an older woman for love. That should be obvious. He's aggressive and ambitious, willing to kill when his career is threatened. Kill four people! He's bold and ruthless. He was sleeping with Samantha to get ahead in the company, pick her brains, learn the company secrets, get the inside dope.

"And now she thought he belonged to *her*. And she was going to make sure he didn't stray. So back she came to keep him away from Roxanne. And he's not about to put up with that sort of thing. He's killed three. Why not make it four and clear the decks? She was a threat while she lived, anyway. Even if she shared his guilt, she might pull them both down if she got mad enough or desperate enough. And he doesn't like to be beaten. I think the idea of having to stand by and let Neville beat him out with Roxanne galled the hell out of him."

Dagger pointed. Peter and Roxanne were watching together a big, graying grandfather baboon pacing back and forth on the grass about fifteen yards off the path while Neville had placed himself on Roxanne's other side, within reaching but not touching distance. "Look at that," the colonel said. "Neville's been squeezed out. Peter knows all the moves. By tomorrow, Neville won't even be in sight."

Lumumba, observing the trio, said, "American women don't get to choose for themselves, do they?"

"Oh, yes," Dagger said. "My daughter makes all her own decisions. I worry because she isn't married, but now I think maybe it's because she isn't gullible. Maybe I should worry if she were quick into wedlock. She scared me in the beginning, when Peter and Neville gave her the big rush, but she doesn't care about either of those two men. I can tell. She's just standing still, letting them play their games, watching, waiting, smiling, for some secret reason of her own. But never mind her. The guy with her is your murderer, Captain."

"Yes," Lumumba answered. "But the clues are subtle. I don't think there's anything we can hold him for."

"How about suspicion, Captain? Slam him behind bars, then gather the evidence. There's a wristwatch around Lake Baringo that belongs to him. There are liquor stores in town here and Père Javineau liqueur is so special, a clerk might remember who bought a bottle. And his clothes, under a microscope, might reveal threads from the dress Samantha was wearing when she died."

"Yes," Captain Lumumba answered. "An arrest is in order. Thank you for your help, Colonel."

"My pleasure."

"Shall we?"

The three of us moved over to Roxanne and Peter, standing a bit apart from the others in the group watching the pacing baboon. As Peter turned at our arrival, Lumumba clamped his shoulder with his large hand. "You're under arrest for murder," he said.

THIRTY-ONE

Tuesday, July 1

I SUPPOSE WE ALL expected Peter Tower, first, to gape at Lumumba, second, profess innocence, and third, in outrage deny everything. What he did, instead, was turn at the clap on Lumumba's hand upon his shoulder, and with a speed that showed he'd planned it in advance, snatched the pistol from Lumumba's left holster and, pulling Roxanne with him, back off, holding us all at bay.

"Oh no you don't," he announced, keeping to a safe distance. The others in the group were up ahead on the path watching and feeding the baboons, and only Neville realized what was going on. Behind, the path to the vans was empty. Out on the grassy fields, only the big graying baboon paid attention. The rest were holding out paws to the tourists for bread. Two policemen armed with rifles were with the group and they turned, but Peter was watching them and his gun was aimed at Lumumba's chest.

"Tell them to drop those rifles," Peter ordered the police captain, and Lumumba spoke to them over his shoulder. They let their rifles drop.

"You aren't going to throw me in your lousy jails," Peter told the captain. "You aren't going to leave me there to rot. I saw the three of you talking. I knew what you were talking about. I saw you start over here. I didn't know what you had on me, but I knew you had it figured and I wasn't going to stand still and wait to be arrested. Now I'm getting out of here and I've got a hostage to prove it." He indicated Roxanne, whose upper arm was gripped by his iron fingers. She was white of face, but composed.

There were gasps and cries from the rest of the group. They all now realized that Peter Tower was aiming a gun at big Captain Lumumba, and that he held Roxanne Dagger prisoner with his other hand.

Peter gestured with the gun and announced loudly, "Roxanne and I are going back to America on the next flight out, Lumumba, and you're going to make all the arrangements. Put your hands on your head, you black bastard, and get over here. You're going to drive us to the airport and see that we get safely aboard the plane. And you're going to arrange for our safe landing back home. You're going to let all the authorities everywhere know that a woman's life is at stake."

Peter backed a couple of steps toward the nearest van, but Lumumba didn't move. Peter stopped and a scowl darkened his face. He raised his voice. "Did you hear me, you son of a bitch? Get in that van!"

"You let that girl go," Lumumba answered, "and we'll go easy with you."

Peter leveled his gun. "You think I won't shoot you? Killing an arrogant, uppity bastard like you would make my day." He gestured with his gun at the vans behind him. "You get one more chance before I put a hole in that pretty uniform you wear."

"Let that girl go," Lumumba roared.

Peter fired and Lumumba took a half step back, staggering slightly. He went for his other gun, the one in his right holster. Peter fired again and a woman screamed. This time Lumumba fell. I tried to catch him, but I couldn't hold him, could only ease him down. Blood was starting to stain the front of his uniform.

Peter positioned Roxanne as a shield and pressed the muzzle of his gun against Roxanne's temple again. He took one backward glance to get his bearings, and moved to the van. And suddenly, on top of the van, there appeared the big graying baboon. Amram saw him and paused. Peter, with one arm around Roxanne's neck, gestured impatiently with the gun. "Come on. You want this girl to die? Get moving." Then the baboon jumped onto Peter's back and sank his teeth into his throat.

Peter dropped Roxanne and dropped the gun. He clawed with both hands at the powerful, hairy brute that had sprung upon him. But it was only for a moment. His grip weakened and his legs buckled and the baboon sprang free. Then Peter was down on the path on his back and his arms fell lifeless and outstretched, his throat torn out so that only the spine connected head to body, and the blood gushed out in dying spurts around him while the baboon went scampering away for the trees.

Roxanne, who was closest, stared at the dead man in horror and turned away. Amram, who was next closest, remarked almost laconically, "Baboons have good memories. That's the baboon Mr. Tower fed hot pepper to ten days ago."

COLONEL DAGGER was at Lumumba's side, propping his head. "You shouldn't have fought him," he gently told the police captain, the stain on whose uniform was growing larger and larger. "You should've done as he said."

"You helped me," the large police captain grunted. "I may not be worthy of this uniform, but I could not let him kidnap your daughter." He tried to look around. "Is she all right?"

Roxanne knelt beside him and said she was fine. "A baboon came to the rescue. It killed him and saved me."

"I'm glad the Kenyan animals could do for you what the people could not."

Lumumba's two policemen were at his side now, talking with Lumumba and the drivers, arranging to get him to the hospital. Dagger told Lumumba he was going with him, too, to make sure the authorities understood that he'd been shot while arresting the man who'd committed the four murders. Lumumba said it was not proper, that the colonel deserved the credit. Dagger answered with a firm "No," and Lumumba could not quarrel. He was losing consciousness.

"Look after Roxanne," Dagger told me. "I'll be back when I can."

THIRTY-TWO

THE COLONEL, Captain Lumumba, one policeman, and Amram as driver, went off in the first van. An anxious Roxanne made her father promise to phone as soon as he had word on Captain Lumumba's condition.

The second policeman stood guard over Peter's body and the rest of us, in shocked silence, were transported back to the Nairobi Sabrina Hotel.

Roxanne stayed with me in the suite I shared with Dagger, waiting word, and she paced the floor to and fro, sharing some of her father's Scotch with me. "Poor Captain Lumumba," she kept saying. "He shouldn't have done it for me. Peter couldn't hold out forever. He'd have to sleep."

I said I thought Lumumba felt he had to do it, that it was a matter of honor.

"You men and your honor, or pride, or whatever," she answered, shaking her head. "I wonder any of you survive." She freshened her drink and stared into the glass. "What do you think, James? Do you think he was losing an awful lot of blood? His uniform was terribly stained. I don't want him dying on my account. I wouldn't want to have to live with that. What do you think his chances are?"

I said I thought he'd come through all right, but she knew I was telling her what she wanted to hear and I don't think she believed me.

We were an hour in the room, with Roxanne's thoughts on Captain Lumumba. All she said about Peter was to thank God baboons had good memories and a desire to get even.

Then the phone rang and she snatched it up. Her back was to me and I couldn't tell from the cock of her head or position of her body, or from the inflection in her voice, what the answer was. Not until the end, when she gave a little shriek of joy and hung up. "Superficial!" she said, turning around with a glorious smile. "The first bullet went through his shoulder. The second, lower down, was deflected by his medals and isn't serious."

"Hurray," I said, and kissed her. I figured that was a good excuse and I'd been wanting to do it ever since I first set eyes on her. She didn't draw away like a frightened doe and it felt so good, I kissed her again, lingeringly this time.

"What's that all about?" she said, looking up at me in wonder.

"Celebrating Captain Lumumba's condition," I answered.

"I mean the second kiss."

"I couldn't resist. I've been wanting to do that ever since we met."

"You could've fooled me," she replied. "I didn't think you even knew I was alive."

"You were so busy with Peter and Neville I didn't have a chance."

"You noticed?"

"Noticed? I couldn't take my eyes off you. I was jealous as hell!"

"My goodness," she said. She put her hands on my cheeks, and kissed me on the mouth. "Don't tell me it worked?"

"What worked?"

"That's exactly what I wanted you to be—jealous as hell. But I didn't think you noticed. I gave up thinking you'd notice."

"You mean that Peter-Neville business was for my benefit?"

"Well, how else do you think I could attract the attention of a man who writes articles about Manhattan as a bachelor's paradise? If I made a frontal assault, I'd end up as just another scalp on your belt."

I think I flushed a little. "I want you to know that not all the material in that article was acquired firsthand."

"Nevertheless, I was intimidated. And I was damned if I was going to make a fool of myself." She smiled. "So there you have it."

I pulled her to me and kissed her again, and this time she wrapped her long arms around me and kissed me back. When we broke, she said, "One thing. If the next thing you say is 'Your room or mine,' I'll never speak to you again."

"I wasn't going to say that," I answered. "I was thinking of something more old-fashioned, like 'I love you.'"

"Those are the kind of words a woman really likes to hear."

We kissed again and I said, "In fact, what comes to mind is something very traditional, like 'Will you marry me?'"

"After only knowing me ten days?"

"How long am I supposed to know you?"

She laughed. "Before you take it back, the answer is yes. It was 'yes' the moment I first set eyes on you, as you can tell by the elaborate game I played to get you. But I wanted to make sure *you* were sure."

"I'm sure."

WE WERE STILL in each other's arms when Dagger came back. He entered the room and stopped dead. We both turned, I flushing, Roxanne giving him her sunburst smile. "Papa," she said, "I have to correct what you told Jim last week. You were wrong when you said I was the one and only girl who wasn't looking for a husband from the age of fourteen on. I was too looking! It just took me longer to find one."

"Husband?" Dagger inquired, and planted both hands on his cane.

"Jim and I are going to get married. Husband and wife! I do hope you won't mind him for a son-in-law."

He looked from one of us to the other. "How long has this been going on?"

"Since we all met together in the Iberia waiting room back at JFK." She went to him and planted a big kiss on his cheek. "Hah," she said. "A fine detective *you* are!"

Worldwide Mysteries—keeping you in suspense with award-winning authors.

Can you keep a secret?

You can keep this one plus 2 free novels.